HOT SHOTS

By the same author

The Goldfish Bowl

Death on a No. 8 Hook

HOT SHOTS

a novel

by

Laurence Gough

LONDON
VICTOR GOLLANCZ LTD
1989

First published in Great Britain 1989
by Victor Gollancz Ltd,
14 Henrietta Street, London WC2E 8QJ

British Library Cataloguing in Publication Data
Gough, Laurence
Hot shots.
I. Title
813′.54[F]

ISBN 0–575–04516 7

Typeset at The Spartan Press Ltd,
Lymington, Hants
Printed in Great Britain by St Edmundsbury Press Ltd,
Bury St Edmunds, Suffolk

This one is for my father, W. C. B.

1

Gary Silk was down eight points. He was about as angry as a man with everything can be. Because he'd lost his temper he'd lost his rhythm. His timing was all shot to hell. He was disgusted with himself, the way he was running all over the damn court, bouncing off the walls with his damn tongue hanging out, trying to get something going against the pro's barrage of stupid little dinky lob shots. He knew what he was doing wrong — chasing the goddamn ball instead of working the court, letting the ball come to him — but he was out of control, couldn't help himself.

He watched the ball hit the far wall about an eighth of an inch above the foul line and drop straight down. Hit the deck and just lay there, dead. He glared at the pro's broad and muscular back as the golden jerk wound up and fired a bullet into the corner, the little blue sphere caroming off the wall almost at right angles, an impossible shot to return, the ball hitting the adjoining wall before Gary had time to react, then dribbling along the baseboard as if it'd had all the air let out of it.

Now Gary was down nine points.

He jogged over and retrieved the ball, bent from the waist and scooped it up, his knees locked and his skinny hairless legs perfectly straight. Thirty-seven years old but he was in the best shape of his life. Well, why not? He played squash three times a week. Every second day he laced on a hundred-dollar pair of Nikes and put a minimum ten miles on the odometer of his silver Mercedes 560SL convertible, Frank cruising along maybe a hundred feet behind him, one hand draped across the wheel and the other on his gun.

Plus didn't he spend at least an hour a day in the gym, working out on his Universal, which the salesman had told him was the exact same model Clint Eastwood had out at his spread in Carmel?

Gary used his wristband to wipe his forehead dry. He twirled his racket in the air. The pro was watching him out of the corner of his big blue eye, wary, wondering if maybe he'd gone a little too far. Gary gave him a big smile and the pro relaxed, his shoulders dropping. Gary could be a charmer when he was in the mood — people who'd met him said he could charm the teeth out of a doberman, and it was almost true.

He started back down the court, polished maple squeaking under his shoes. The pro stood there, waiting, examining some tiny imagined flaw in the strings of his racket.

So intent was Gary on his game that he had walked almost all the way down the court before he noticed Frank sitting on the edge of his seat on the other side of the glass wall that separated the back of the court from the spectator's area. What was Frank up to? He was no sports fan, and anyway knew it was the pro's job to beat the shit out of Gary, make him, in theory, a better player. Frank was smart enough not to hang around and watch Gary get thumped.

Clearly, Frank's presence had to be bad news. Gary tossed the ball to the pro, flipping it underhand, but putting a little extra zip on it.

"Gotta run. Let's call it a draw, okay?"

"Sure thing, Mr Silk." The pro gave Gary his very best smile. The kid had teeth like fucking Chicklets, so white they looked like he'd stuck tiny hundred-watt light bulbs in them. He hustled over to the small square door set flush into the back wall of the court, below where the glass started. He yanked the door open and stepped aside. Gary stooped and slipped through, into the locker room.

Frank trotted down the stairs from the gallery. He didn't say anything, but he looked worried, his eyes a little closer together than usual.

"What?" said Gary.

Frank eyed the pro.

Gary picked up a thick white towel with his initials stitched into one corner in shiny purple thread. He snapped the towel playfully at Frank's crotch. "Give him fifty."

The pro mumbled his gratitude. Fifty bucks an hour for doing something he was good at and probably spent a lot of time doing for nothing anyway, simply because he liked it, the game was fun. Probably thought the fifty was easy money, life was a fucking bowl of maraschino cherries.

Frank snapped three crisp twenties out of his wallet. "Got a ten?" he said to the pro, offering him the money.

The pro made a big production of going through his wallet, his pockets. Nothing. He started fooling with his bright red Adidas sports bag, pushing around a bunch of damp towels and unwashed clothes.

Frank waited patiently, not saying anything even though the guy was obviously broke.

Finally the pro zipped up his bag of dirty laundry, glanced at Gary, shrugged and smiled.

"You cut us short," Gary said to Frank. "We only played what, about half an hour? Maybe fifty's too much, twenty would be more reasonable." Gary paused, letting the suspense build and the pro squirm. "But what the hell, right? Guy rode all the way over here on a fucking bicycle. And wasn't he ready to play? Wasn't he ready to do his job?"

The pro made a grab for the money. Frank, sweetheart that he was, let him have it.

"Thank you, Mr Silk," the pro said.

Gary nodded. In five years the sucker's smile would be all worn out, his reflexes gone. He'd have a bad case of melanoma from too many summers in the sun, too many winters spent under the heat lamps. What then? With no education and no street smarts, he'd be lucky to get a job washing dishes.

"Same time next Friday?" The pro tucked the money into the key pocket of his shorts, screwing up his face as he worked at the flap.

"Maybe," said Gary vaguely. "I could be outta town on Friday. Do a long weekend, y'know? Miami, or maybe Vegas." He shrugged. "Let's leave it like this — plan to be here but be ready to get cancelled. Okay?"

"Sure," said the pro. Gary was trying to think of his name. Peter something. Disappointment was smeared all over his face.

Gary felt a bit better, like he'd rallied, picked up a few late points. He liked to keep the people around him a little off balance. It was a habit, something he worked at automatically without even thinking about it. He strongly believed that the art of living was at least ninety percent habit. If you had good habits, you enjoyed a good life. You developed bad habits, you were fucked. Of course it wasn't quite as simple as that.

There was a kicker, as always.

Because good habits didn't matter one way or the other if you were the kind of person who didn't know how to deal with the other ten percent of life — the shit that popped up when you least expected it, and had to be dealt with quickly and correctly.

"Mind if I stick around and take a quick shower?" said the pro.

Gary glanced at Frank. Frank's face said no. The pro zipped up his bright red Adidas bag and Frank showed him the door.

"So what the hell is it?" said Gary as he and Frank walked along the heated, glass-enclosed passageway that connected the squash courts and gymnasium to the main house.

Frank cleared his throat. Frank was six four and two hundred and seventy pounds, hard as a brick. Gary Silk stood five foot six in those bright red iguana-skin high-heeled cowboy boots he liked to wear, and he weighed in at maybe a hundred and forty pounds, including a three-piece suit with a silk hankie, pocketful of change and fully loaded Smith and Wesson .357 Magnum stainless tucked away in a back pocket.

Gary liked to think of himself as a John McEnroe type. He had the same lean and compact body, pale eyes that never seemed to blink. He also had, Frank had to hand it to him, an overpowering intensity of purpose.

The big difference was, McEnroe swatted tennis balls and Gary swatted people. He scared the living shit right out of Frank, and Frank was secure enough about himself so he didn't care who knew it.

Gary reached up and playfully bounced the flat of his racket off the top of Frank's head. Frank favoured a brushcut. His hair went flat and then sprang back.

"C'mon, give," said Gary. "What's going on?"

"Pat Nash and Oscar Peel just showed up," said Frank. "Parked out on the street by the gate, right in front of the house. Walked up the driveway and here they are."

"What about the dogs?"

"They're at the vet's."

"Yeah, right." Gary smirked, remembering. He was hard on animals. They came, suffered, disappeared. "You got somebody keeping tabs on our two guests, make sure they don't pinch the silverware?"

Frank nodded, not meeting Gary's eye. Gary bounced the racket off Frank's head again, a little harder this time. The strings made a sound that was almost musical.

"What the fuck they doing here, Frank?"

"I didn't ask."

Gary's mind raced. "They clean?"

"Spotless."

"What kind of car they drive up in?"

"Beats me. Like I told you, they left it down by the front gate."

Gary picked up the pace. They reached the end of the walkway. Frank stepped in front of Gary and pushed open the door, which was made of heavy gauge steel plate with a thin oak veneer. There was the mud room, and then the huge kitchen, all copper and chrome, gleaming white tile.

A video camera equipped with a wide-angle lens and heat-activated tracking device followed their progress across the room. Another camera picked them up as they passed through double swinging doors and started down the wide central hallway that bisected the house. There was a six-foot barrel cactus in a big clay pot. Gary paused to check the soil. Nice and dry.

"Where are they, in the living-room?"

Frank shook his head. "The den. I turned on the fireplace."

Gary nodded. "You're a good host, Frank. A real peach of a guy."

2

Detective Jack Willows sat on the edge of his bed with the telephone in his lap. He dialled a one to get long distance, then four-zero-six, the area code for Toronto, and finally his father-in-law's number.

The phone rang twice and then the answering machine picked up. He was invited to leave a message. There was an unspoken option, of course. Willows took it. He slammed down the phone and carried his lowball glass back into the kitchenette for a refill.

3

There was dark oak paneling on both sides of the hallway, a pale shipdeck oak floor. Recessed pot lights to highlight the quartet of Chick Rice portraits Gary had commissioned.

When Gary was drunk or maybe a little coked up he often asked Frank what he thought of the photographs. Frank always said he thought they were terrific, which was a lie.

Kind of a lie.

Fact was, Frank thought the pictures were fantastic, sensational. They were true to Gary and yet at the same time subtly flattered him, managed to project him in a good light. But, and Frank had no idea how this was accomplished, the portraits also somehow managed to show the real Gary, the nasty, vindictive little dink that lurked under the thirty-dollar haircut and twice-weekly facials.

Frank was sure that Gary had no idea just how good Chick Rice's portraits were, which was fine with him, because if Gary ever did wise up, the pictures would hit the fireplace and Frank would probably have to waste a couple of days convincing him it wasn't such a hot idea to bump off a high-profile photographer.

In the entrance hall, stained-glass panels on either side of the big front door sparkled under the lights of the chandelier. Gary paused at a small alcove beside the wide, curving staircase that led to the second floor. In the alcove there was a reproduction Queen Anne table with a Princess phone on it, and a brass pot with three legs made out of clenched fists. The pot contained a cactus that bloomed red flowers at Christmas time. Gary had a thing about cactuses; the weird prickly plants were all over the house. Frank had stuck himself more than once.

On the wall directly behind the table hung an oval bevelled-glass mirror.

Gary peered into the mirror, checking himself out. He took off his diagonal-striped blue and white headband. The strip of elasticized cloth had left a broad red streak across the pale flesh of his forehead. He scrubbed himself with the palm of his hand but the mark wouldn't go away. He put the headband back on, curled his lip. He looked sort of piratical. Maybe it wasn't so bad after all.

"I look like a pirate, Frank?"

"Sure thing, Gary."

Gary laughed, openly admired his teeth in the mirror.

They went up the stairs and along a hallway, past a number of closed doors. The house was three storeys high, a little under ten thousand square feet. On the second floor there were six bedrooms and five bathrooms and the den. The den was down at the far end of the house. It was one of Gary's favorite rooms, because the windows overlooked his backyard acreage; the glassed-in pool and tennis and squash courts, the maze and solar-heated greenhouse, vegetable garden. Frank opened the door and they went into the den. Frank shut the door behind them and leaned against it.

Pat Nash and Oscar Peel were standing on the tiled hearth in front of the fire. They were both naked.

Peel's hands were cupped protectively over his crotch but Nash was warming his hands, holding them out to the flames. Nash had hair all over his body. He looked to Gary like a goddamn animal that had learned to stand on its hind legs. Peel was almost hairless except for a scrawny moustache and the hair on his head, which was reddish blond and swept straight back. Both men turned towards Gary as he came into the room. Nash said hello and put his hands on his hips. Peel kept his mouth shut, which was a point in his favor.

Gary looked at Pat Nash as if Nash was a guest at the city pound and Gary was thinking about maybe getting himself a new pet.

"What's in the car?" Gary said to Nash. "Why'd you leave it out on the street?"

"Nothing, Mr Silk."

"Excuse me?"

"The car's empty. It's hot, is all."

"Hot in here, too," said Oscar Peel. He licked his lips, moved a little way away from the fireplace, bare feet silent on the tiles.

"Get back where you were," said Frank.

"I'm gonna fry my ass," said Peel. But he did what he was told.

"We lost the shipment," said Nash.

"Bullshit."

"What happened . . ." said Peel.

Gary took three quick strides across the red and blue and gold Star Usak carpet and slashed at him with his racket. Peel's head snapped back. He grunted with pain. A line of blood rose up across his cheekbone, just below his left eye. He lifted his hand to touch the wound and Gary reared back and hit him again, swiped viciously at him, the graphite racket making a hissing noise in the air. Peel screamed as the racket chopped him across the bridge of the nose.

"Hurts, does it?" said Gary.

Peel groaned and dropped to one knee.

"Get up," said Frank.

Peel dragged himself upright. Blood splattered from his broken nose to the priceless sixteenth-century carpet. He cupped his hands under his nose and stood motionless, his manhood shrunken with fear.

Gary poked at his groin with the handle of the racket, sadly shook his head. "What'd you do when you're horny, grease a thimble?"

Frank chuckled.

"Was that funny, Frank?"

"Really funny."

"Am I good enough for the Catskills?"

"Almost," said Frank.

Gary mimed bashing him with the racket. Went over to the bar and yanked open the fridge, grabbed himself a beer. Lost electrolytes and maybe eighty million dollars worth of heroin were leading him straight down the road into migraine country. He popped the cap off the beer and threw the cap at Oscar Peel.

He grinned at Pat Nash. "Before I kill you, I'm gonna give you a chance to tell me what happened. Fair enough?"

Nash looked at Oscar Peel, whose hands were filled and overflowing with blood.

Gary drank some beer. He glanced at Frank, to make sure he was paying attention. Gary had a feeling that before the night was over, somebody was going to die. Since he liked to think he was an equal opportunity employer, he wanted to make sure he got it right. "What the fuck you waiting for?" he yelled at Nash.

Nash jumped. "Everything went real smooth at first. We offloaded from the tender at eleven o'clock sharp, no problem."

Gary nodded. The heroin, smack, white lady, call it what you wanted, had come in on a Japanese freighter full of shiny new cars. It was a regular run; they'd used it before and never had any problems.

"There was a lot of fog," said Nash. "It was so thick you couldn't see the end of the fucking boat. We came in along English Bay, went past the Coast Guard wharf and under the bridge. We could see lights on the wharf, but nothing else. We were coming in real easy. At the bridge the channel gets narrower. We had to give the engine more power, because of the tide."

"The current there gets pretty strong," said Peel. The bleeding had stopped but his head was still bowed and his nose was full of congealed blood. It was hard for Gary to understand what he was saying. He gave Frank a look.

Frank said, "Shut your fuckin' mouth, Oscar."

"We were worried about the Coast Guard," said Nash. "But it was the city cops that spotted us. We didn't hear their engines or even see them until they were right on top of us. Coming right at us, you know? Guy up on the bridge yellin' at us through a megaphone, we couldn't understand a fuckin' word."

"Twenty kilos of ninety percent pure," said Silk. "Don't tell me you already made bail."

"We chucked the dope overboard," said Pat Nash.

Gary struggled to control his temper. He went over to the window and looked out at his floodlit backyard, the vegetable patch enclosed with netting to keep out the birds.

"Why didn't you run for it? Dincha have the brains to figure, in the darkness, if you couldn't see them, they wouldn't be able to see you?"

Nobody said anything.

"There's eighty million of my dollars sitting on the bottom of the harbor, is that what you're telling me?"

"That's retail," cautioned Frank.

Gary ignored him.

"It was in a plastic garbage bag," said Nash. "A dark green one, sealed with that silvery tape they use for duct pipe."

"*Duct pipe*? What the fuck is that? What the fuck you talking about?"

"It's out there somewhere," said Nash. "The tide would've carried it right out of the harbor."

"Eighty million bucks. What am I supposed to do, take it out of your allowance?"

Frank laughed and Silk glared at him. Frank studied the shifting flames in the gas fireplace, looking for a pattern.

"They had us in the fucking bag," Nash said. His voice was low, calm, unhurried. "Anybody would've dumped the stuff. Twenty kilos, Jesus. We'd of gone down for life."

Gary smiled. "Could work out that way anyhow, the way I see it."

"With all due respect, Mr Silk, what would you have done?"

"Something different. Something a whole lot smarter. What happened after you deep-sixed my drugs?"

"Nothing," said Pat Nash. "The cops just veered away. It turned out what they were yelling was that we didn't have any running lights."

"Which one of you assholes actually grabbed the bag and threw it overboard?"

There was a pause, an ominous silence that was broken only by the thick wet sound of a drop of Oscar Peel's blood hitting the tile hearth. And then Pat Nash said, "I did. It was my decision."

Gary said, "Put your clothes on, both of you."

While they were getting dressed, Gary went over to the bar and grabbed himself another beer. Pat Nash had been wearing knee-length black leather boots and dark green wide-wale cords, a black leather jacket. Oscar Peel had dressed less formally — faded Levis and a thick green and black plaid workshirt, a yellow rain slicker, black sneakers.

"Take 'em back to the beach," Gary told Frank. He pointed at Pat Nash. "Find someplace nice and quiet and leave him there."

"What about him?" said Frank, pointing his Colt at Oscar Peel.

"Oscar can pull the trigger, then go find my drugs." Gary smiled. "That okay with you, Oscar?"

"Me'n Pat have been partners for years, Mr Silk. I mean, he's almost my fucking brother-in-law, I'm married to his cousin."

"Do both of them," Gary said to Frank.

Frank nodded. He waved the Colt. "Let's hit the road, fellas."

"You wanna take somebody else along, give you a hand?" said Gary.

Frank gave Gary a look. Three years together and he still couldn't tell when Gary was serious and when he was pulling his leg. "I'll be okay," Frank said.

Gary shrugged.

"I'm a married man," said Oscar Peel. "I got a wife, a nice apartment . . ."

Silk turned to Pat Nash. "What about you, got any dependents?"

Nash shook his head.

"Your choice," Silk said to Oscar Peel. "You do Pat or Frank shoots both of you."

Oscar Peel wiped his bloody hands together. He made a whining noise.

"What?" said Gary.

Peel nodded his head.

"Is that a yes?"

Oscar mumbled something.

"Louder," said Gary.

"Yes," whispered Oscar Peel.

Gary anointed him with the racket. "You'll shoot the fucker?"

"Yes," said Oscar, not much louder. He wiped his upper lip and his nose started bleeding again.

"Right now, right this minute?" Gary's eyes were hot and moist. Oscar stared at the carpet. "Don't anybody move," said Gary.

Gary hurried out of the den, leaving the door open behind him. Frank kept his Colt steady on Nash and Peel. The gas flames licked at the ceramic logs. They could all hear Gary out in the hall, whistling cheerfully. He was gone less than a minute and when he came back he was carrying a small automatic, a purse gun, a .25 calibre Star. He drew back the slide, let go. Now there was a round in the chamber. All you had to do was pull the trigger. He ejected the clip into the palm of his hand, tossed the weapon to Oscar Peel.

"Keep an eye on him, Frank."

"You betcha."

Frank moved around behind Peel and Nash. He brought the Colt up suddenly and backhanded Nash across the side of the head. Nash dropped to his knees. Frank grabbed his hair and held him upright. "Do it, Oscar."

"You got one shot," said Silk. "Get in nice and close. Stick the barrel right up his ear." Gary clapped his hands together. "Bang! You got him. See how easy it is?"

Pat Nash groaned. His eyes fluttered.

Oscar Peel edged a little closer. He told himself he was five years younger than Pat, that he was married and had a wife and baby and probably since Nash smoked two packs a day the guy was dying of cancer anyway, and he was doing him a favor, putting him out of his misery. None of it worked. He made his mind go blank. Gripping the little gun in both hands, he aimed at the back of Pat Nash's head, inched close enough to touch the front sight against the top of his skull, where the hair formed a little whirlpool.

"I'm sorry," he whispered.

"Tell it like it is," said Gary, and patted him on the back.

"Fuck the both of you," said Nash, his voice thick with pain.

Oscar pulled the trigger. The gun clicked as the hammer fell on an empty chamber.

Gary reached over Peel's shoulder, yanked the gun away from him. "You'd shoot your own brother-in-law? You fucking hump!" Gary started hitting him with the edge of the racket. Peel retreated, stumbled, fell back. His arm swept half a dozen trophies from the fireplace mantle. Gary screamed with rage. The racket slammed into Peel's back, Gary dealing a series of two-handed blows, going for the spine.

"Pick 'em up! Pick 'em up!"

Peel scrambled across the floor. Gary kept hitting him as he put the trophies back on the mantle. Peel's nose had started bleeding again and there was more blood on his temple and behind his ear, angry red welts across his back.

Gary pushed him out of the way. He went over to Pat Nash, knelt down so they were on a level. He pulled back the Star's slide, slipped a round into the breech and jammed the gun into the breast pocket of Nash's jacket. The leather creaked.

"Your turn now," said Gary. "Your turn if you wanna take it."

Oscar was leaning against the wall, crying.

At a motion from Gary, Frank took Nash by the arm and helped him to his feet.

Gary reached up and stroked Nash's cheek. "Same deal. Either he goes or you both go. And you got three days to get my dope back for me or Frank's gonna come after you. Kill you, understand?"

Nash nodded wearily. Oscar was still crying. The way he was going, might never get a chance to stop.

"I'm gonna take a shower and then go to bed and watch some TV," Gary said to Frank. "Lemme know when you get back, okay? So I don't stay up all night worrying."

"Okay," said Frank.

Oscar started yelling at Gary Silk, but he was crying so hard that Silk couldn't understand a goddamn word he was saying. It was like baby talk. Gibberish. What the guy needed was an interpreter. And somebody to wipe his nose. Gary handed something to Frank. A wide roll of adhesive tape. Frank grabbed a fistful of hair and held Peel still while he wound the tape around and around his head. Peel was still crying, but silently now, snorting blood.

Pat Nash was something else again. Gary admired him, the way he was standing there, quiet and waiting, like he was memorizing everything, just taking it all in. For a fleeting moment, Gary thought maybe it would be a good idea to bump Nash off, too. But business was, like they said, business.

And if he didn't get the heroin back, wouldn't it be nice to have somebody handy to pound into mush?

Pat Nash would do just fine.

4

Constables Paul Lambert and Chris Furth were having a good shift. Late August, and you couldn't ask more of the weather — blue skies and light winds. It was early, just a few minutes past seven. The temperature was already in the low seventies, but the commuters hadn't started to clog the streets yet, and the air was still fresh and pure. They'd worked their way almost to the end of shift, and hadn't yet been assaulted by a drunk or a whore or a lunatic. None of their arrests had thought to toss his cookies in the back seat of the squad car. And better yet, they'd had a long, emotionally satisfying discussion about baseball in general and the fate of the Blue Jays in particular.

All in all, a more or less perfect shift.

Except of course for the usual argument about where to eat breakfast.

"I want some McNuggets."

"Nobody eats McNuggets for breakfast, Lambert."

"I do. With sweet and sour sauce." Lambert's hard leather handcuff case was digging into the small of his back. Sometimes he truly believed that the police uniform with all its cumbersome and unwieldy equipment had been designed primarily to improve the force's posture. He sat a little straighter in his seat.

"Let's eat at Juanita's."

"They don't open until eleven."

"For us, they will."

Furth made a face. "Tacos for breakfast? Forget it." Juanita's was a Mexicalifornian fast food joint. Lambert was renowned for his voracious appetite and ability to eat anything, while Furth had a notoriously weak stomach.

"Why don't we flip for it, let Lady Luck decide?"

Furth gave Lambert a suspicious look. "My coin or yours?"

"Whatever."

Furth searched his pockets and found a quarter. He balanced the coin on his thumbnail, which was bitten to the quick. "Call it in the air."

"Go ahead."

Furth levered the coin into the air. It hit the roof liner and ricocheted to the floor.

"Tails," said Lambert.

Furth retrieved the coin, scowled.

At Juanita's, Furth hadn't been able to bring himself to eat anything except a few taco chips and a taste of salsa. But that left all the more for Lambert, who patted his stomach, burped heartily, sipped his Perrier and wished he was a detective so he could drink beer on the job without anybody knowing about it.

Lambert glanced around the restaurant, taking in the décor. There was a great big happy sun that bulged out of the wall. The sun was made out of plaster painted bright yellow. There was also a pale blue fingernail moon and a bunch of shiny silver stars made out of jumbo paperclips that had been bent into shape.

Everywhere you looked, there were groupings of tiny papier mâché figures with pink faces and small black eyes. The figures were comical, but somehow very human. Lambert admired the artists' ability to fashion the characters so they were primitive and sophisticated all at the same time. He waved at the owner, a dark, grossly underweight man with a black moustache shaped like wings, and eyes that never stopped smiling.

"What d'we owe you, pal?"

The man made a gesture of dismissal. "Nothing, not a single peso. Your company is my reward."

"On the house, you mean?" Lambert frowned. "I can't let you do that, it wouldn't be right."

"True," said Furth.

Lambert glared at him. Furth stared unblinkingly back. Finally Lambert reached for his wallet. He flipped it open, studied the contents with astonishment. "Jeez, I thought I had a twenty. Mind if I catch you next time, amigo?"

*

Furth unlocked the blue and white Aspen, got inside and reached across to let Lambert into the car. Lambert worked his mint-flavored toothpick.

"Why do you *do* that?"

"So I won't get cavities."

"No, I mean why do you always go through that charade with Juanita, or whatever the hell his name is. He'll never get a dime or a peso or a goddamn bus token out of you, and you both know it."

"Mexicans are a very polite people," Lambert said. "You have to respect their customs." He spat a fragment of green pepper out the window, burped noisily and sighed with pleasure.

Furth drove the Aspen east on Robson, past the trendy boutiques and expensive men's wear shops, multitude of ethnic restaurants and the weird little places that sold cookies by the ounce. The Art Gallery. Law Courts and Robson Square. He hit Granville and turned right. It was quarter to eight. The sun was higher and it was getting hotter, traffic was thick. Lambert rolled his window up, fighting the diesel fumes. They turned right on Davie and then left on Howe, cut into the inside lane and dipped down past the Howe Street access ramp to the Granville Street Bridge, the main access route from the south side of the city to the downtown core.

Lambert tried to force another burp. He adjusted his seat belt so it wasn't pressing so hard on his belly. Four enchiladas and two large orders of refried beans on top of all those tacos and salsa plus a handful of the mean as hell little green peppers they served free to get you to drink more beer had encouraged him to down three *muy frio* bottles of Perrier, and now his stomach felt as if he'd swallowed an iceberg big enough to sink the Titanic.

Furth turned left on to Beach. They were directly beneath the bridge now, in deep shadow, the bridge's massive concrete support posts on either side of them. Furth turned right. They cruised slowly towards the water.

"Where we going?" said Lambert.

"Nowhere in particular."

"Why don't we get back in the sun, enjoy it while we can?"

They hit a pothole. The Aspen shuddered and Lambert belched loudly, gave a little gasp of pleasure.

"Only intelligent thing you've said all day," Furth remarked.

Lambert ignored the insult. A pale blue Pontiac had smashed into the last of the huge concrete pillars on their side of the water. Furth spun the wheel. The Aspen's radials crunched across a span of waste ground, a field of unrecognizable chunks of metal and fragments of colored glass.

The back door on the driver's side was wide open but the car was in shadow backlighted by sun-streaked water; it was impossible to see inside.

Furth parked beside and slightly behind the Pontiac. He switched off the engine. He could hear a shrill squealing above the dull thunder of traffic a hundred or more feet over his head. He got out of the car and looked up.

The complex of steel girders supporting the bridge was lined with thousands upon thousands of raucous Japanese starlings. During the 1940s, several hundred of the birds had been imported to eradicate some insect or the other. Now they numbered in the thousands. The birds were hardy enough to stick around during the city's notoriously mild winters, and although work crews with sandblasting equipment were sent out every spring to obliterate their nests, they continued to multiply.

"You coming?" Furth said to Lambert, and slammed shut his door.

Lambert climbed out of the Aspen. The roof of the Pontiac and the ground all around him was splattered with what looked like gobs of whitish-yellow paint. He put on his hat. Better to soil his uniform than the top of his head.

The Pontiac was big, a four-door model from the late sixties. The key was in the ignition, and there were at least a dozen or more other keys on a chrome ring the size of a handcuff. Furth reached out to try the front door on the driver's side.

"Don't touch it," said Lambert.

Furth looked across the roof of the car at him.

Lambert was standing by the open rear door. His hand was on his gun.

"What've you got?" said Furth. Something wet and viscous splattered on the metal roof of the Pontiac. He flinched, jerked his head sideways.

"Take a look."

Furth went around to the far side of the car, glass crunching under his shoes. Lambert stepped away from the open door and Furth leaned into the car, careful not to touch anything. First the smell of blood hit him, and then his eyes adjusted to the dimness and he saw how much of it there was, sprayed all across the dashboard and steering wheel, the inside of the windshield. He stepped quickly away from the car, went back to the Aspen and used the Motorola to call in a possible homicide. Only then did he pop open the Aspen's glove compartment and begin a thorough but unsuccessful search for the package of Tums antacid pills he'd left behind at the end of the previous day's shift.

Gone. Furth slammed shut the Aspen's door. Christ, but cops were a bunch of goddamn thieves!

5

Jack Willows was halfway through his second cup of coffee and most of the way through his Saturday morning copy of the *New York Times* when the telephone rang. He turned the page, a scatter of toast crumbs falling from the paper to his lap. The phone kept ringing. A revival theatre was being torn down and Woody Allen was out with a picket sign. He studied the photograph of the crowd in front of the theatre. Woody must've had his back to the camera.

The ringing stopped.

Willows picked up his coffee cup, a big ceramic mug with an orange cat on it, the cat's fluffy tail wrapped around the length of the handle, big green eyes staring fixedly at a family of mice.

The phone started ringing again. It sounded much louder than before, startled Willows and made him gulp his coffee. He put the mug down on the table and pushed back his chair and went into the bedroom.

"Willows."

"I need you," said Claire Parker. "Can you come over and see me?"

Willows could hear a siren in the background, the static of a car radio.

"Where are you?"

"North end of the Granville Street Bridge, down by the water."

"Twenty minutes," said Willows.

"Just enough time for me to change into something comfortable," said Parker. The siren rose to a shrill scream, died.

At the foot of Granville there was a turnaround with a raised circle of river stones in the middle. Behind the turnaround there was a gravel parking lot surrounded by a chain-link fence with an open gate. There were half a dozen cars in the lot. Narrow access roads led down to a second, lower parking lot. The ground was fairly steep. The two lots were separated by a four-foot drop, sloping ground covered with a scrim of wild grass and weeds. The road on the right was gravel, but on the left there was pavement. Willows turned left, drove down to the second parking lot, past a third lot that was empty except for several large power boats that were up on blocks.

There was another chain-link fence, an open gate that provided access to a coffee shop and the waterfront.

Willows eased the front bumper of the Oldsmobile up against a NO PARKING sign, dropped his sun visor so his POLICE VEHICLE notice was in plain view, got out of the Olds and shut and locked the door.

The lower parking lot was in the shape of an inverted T, and the bottom of the T butted right up against one of the huge concrete columns that supported the deck of the bridge, a hundred feet or more above him. Willows walked past a rusty orange dumpster. Knee-high concrete barriers had been placed around the perimeter of the parking lot, and one of them had stopped a pale blue Pontiac from making the ten-foot drop into the harbor. Willows heard a shrill twittering. He glanced up, frowned.

There were three cars in the parking lot: the squad car and the Pontiac and a brown Oldsmobile Cutlass. The Cutlass had been backed right up against the concrete tower leg. It was a four-door, and the right rear tire was flat. As Willows drew nearer he saw that the car was covered in bird droppings and fragments of undigested red berries. The car had no licence plates. The bird droppings were so thick he couldn't see through the windshield.

He turned his attention to the Pontiac. It was straddling one of the cement barriers and the barrier itself had been pushed badly out of alignment by the force of impact. It looked as if someone had tried to run the car over the barrier and into the water. The attempt had failed, but not by much. The Pontiac was balanced like a teeter-totter, the nose of the car out over the water. A little more speed and momentum would have carried it over the barrier and into the depths.

Willows looked down at the calm, milky-green surface of the water. An iridescent abstract of oil lay quietly on the surface. A foam coffee cup spun slowly in the breeze. Willows fished a bright new penny from his pocket, flipped it into the water. Visibility was five or maybe six feet. He wondered how deep the water was. If the car had vanished beneath the surface, would it ever have been found? He heard the crunch of gravel and glanced up and saw Parker walking towards him. She smiled. He nodded, but didn't say anything.

"Morning, Jack. Hope I didn't get you out of bed."

"Is that what I look like, as if I just climbed out of the sack?"

"How would I know?" said Parker. She gestured towards the Pontiac. "While you were enjoying your nap, somebody got shot to death."

Willows stared at the car.

"I think," she amended. Then added, "All that's missing is the body." She glanced past Willows, out across the water.

Wooden stanchions and bright yellow crime scene tape kept away a gathering crowd of construction workers from a nearby building site, people who worked on the docks or lived in the nearby condominiums. Willows looked for Mel Dutton and saw that he had already positioned himself up on the slope and was using a telephoto lens to discreetly snap candids. Willows tipped one of the stanchions and stepped over the tape, held the tape down for Parker. He followed her to the Pontiac. The passenger-side rear door was open. He tucked his tie into the breast pocket of his jacket to keep it from getting dirty, leaned into the car.

There was blood on the front seat, more blood on the steering wheel and dashboard, blood splashed across the radio and glass of the instrument panel, clots of blood and something else, bone or gristle, sticking to the windshield. There was a lot more blood on the door panel, down low. He could see from the pattern that it had impacted with force. It looked like someone had been shot, all right. But you never knew. Knives were always a popular item. If a major artery had been severed, the effect would have been similar. He said, "Who owns the car?"

Parker closed her notebook, dropped her pen into her purse. "MVD says it's registered in the name of Barry Ulysses Crawford. Mr Crawford is twenty-eight years old and the address MVD gave us is suite two-zero-niner, five-two-six East Eighth Avenue."

"But?" said Willows.

"But at the moment and for the past six months he's been residing at five-seven-zero-zero Royal Oak, in the lovely suburb of Burnaby."

Willows nodded. The address she'd given was of the Lower Mainland Regional Correctional Center, a.k.a. Oakalla Prison.

The interior of the Pontiac was suddenly bathed in a cold white light. Mel Dutton smiled at Willows through a side window. He triggered the electronic flash on his Polaroid CU-5 fixed-focus 'fingerprint' camera, and there was another burst of light.

"Hold it a minute, Mel." Willows took another look around the interior of the car. There was a clump of hair and white splinters of bone on the door panel. And something that glinted beneath the gas pedal — a shiny brass tube wedged between the pedal and floor carpet. He crouched down, peered into the dimness.

The brass tube was a spent .25 calibre cartridge.

The pros liked to use small-calibre automatics filled with hollowpoints, get in close and blast away, three or four shots to the head. More often than not there were no exit wounds. But the bullets packed enough punch to turn the victim's brain to pudding. Willows took a long, slow second look at the splash of blood on the door panel, the bone splinters, hair and fragments of tissue.

There were two more spent cartridges wedged between the cushion and backrest of the front seat. Both of them .45s.

Mel Dutton had capped the Polaroid and switched to his Nikon. "Cheese," he said, and crouched and took a quick candid of Willows glaring at him.

Willows bagged the spent cartridges and went around to the front of the car to see what Parker had found to put in the plastic evidence bags lined up on the Pontiac's hood. There were three bags. The first held a misshapen chunk of lead alloy and the second contained a single black leather glove. Willows picked up the third evidence bag. He held the bag up against a shaft of sunlight that slanted down through the bridge girders, made the chrome grill of the Pontiac sparkle brightly. The bag held a small quantity of dark green plant material that looked like spinach.

"Seaweed," said Parker. "That's what it smells like, anyway. The glove and spent slug were on the ground on the far side of the car. Dutton's already photographed them." She was wearing a plain white blouse and a suit, dark blue with pinstripes. The skirt was pleated, the jacket cut to fit close to her body, but with a little padding in the shoulders. Her hair danced in the wind. The light shining off the water made her eyes seem even darker than usual. Willows thought she might have passed for a banker, if she hadn't had such great legs.

He put the evidence bag back down on the hood and stepped back to take a look at the front of the car. A headlight had been smashed. The bumper had been pushed into the grill, puncturing the radiator. There was a residue of rusty water on the ground. The Pontiac had probably been moving at fifteen or twenty miles an hour when it had hit the concrete barrier. He tried to think how it might have happened, pictured a struggle, the victim grabbing the wheel . . . Maybe the shooting had been an accident, the gun discharging when the Pontiac hit the concrete support column. But that would only explain one shot, and especially not two or more shots from two separate weapons. More likely, the shooting had come first and then the killer had tried to run the Pontiac into the drink. When that hadn't worked he'd dragged the body out of the car and dumped it in the water, hoping the tide would carry it out to sea.

He stepped up on the sagging front bumper, gingerly tested it with his weight. The metal made a creaking sound, but held. He walked across to the far side of the car.

The heel marks leading from the front door across the gravel towards the water were faint but perfectly clear. But whoever had dragged the body to the water's edge had left no footprints, no visible traces. Still, it was always possible the Ident squad would turn something up.

In theory, anyway.

Parker stayed close to Willows as he followed the heel marks down to the water's edge. He could smell her perfume. In the rich, syrupy light of summer's day Parker's skin was flawless and pale, her hair black and glossy as a raven's wing. She caught him looking at her, smiled. Willows gruffly looked away.

A concrete breakwater kept the ocean at bay. A wooden float went all the way around to the far side of the pier. On the other side of the float there was open water and then a small marina, about thirty power and sail boats. Willows looked for signs of life, but the boats were quiet, deserted. He wondered if any of them were liveaboards. There'd be a wharfinger nearby; he'd have to find him and ask.

A tug pushed beneath the bridge, riding an ebb tide towards open water. An enclosed barge rode on the end of a short towline. The barge had no markings, other than an eight-digit number. Willows had no idea what the cargo might be. A man in jeans and a windbreaker came out of the tug's wheelhouse. Willows resisted an impulse to wave. What if he was snubbed? The tug's bow wave made the sailboats shift restlessly. He listened to the musical tinkling of the aluminum rigging, watched the masts sway to and fro.

Across the water, the Granville Island Market was on his right. To his left were the huge concrete holding towers of LaFarge Cement. Another cute place to hide a corpse.

The pools of blood in the car had been a hard, glossy brown. The car's engine had been cold. Willows turned to Parker. "Any thoughts?"

"You could use a haircut."

Willows was wearing a crisp white shirt, tan pants, white leather Stan Smith tennis shoes. He kind of liked his hair a little on the longish side. "I thought it made me look kind of artistic," he said.

"Artistic?"

"Sensitive," Willows explained.

"Oh," said Parker. She watched the flow of water under the bridge. It looked glacial, that milky green. "Barry Crawford," she said. "We ought to check, make sure he really is in the slammer."

"Yeah, I suppose so."

Willows turned and began to walk diagonally across the parking lot.

"Where you going?" said Parker.

"Nowhere in particular."

"I've already been over every square inch of ground," said Parker. "I worked out a grid and went over it with the guys from the squad car. Nothing."

Willows nodded but didn't stop walking. Hands in the back pockets of his pants, head down. He whistled a few notes from an old Beatles tune. Abruptly, the whistling stopped. He took his hands out of his pockets, glanced up at Parker.

"What is it?" Parker hurried over to where Willows was standing. There was a small round hole in the hard-packed ground, as if someone had recently removed a rock about the size of a cigarette package.

"We better get Dutton to take some pictures, Claire."

"Right," said Parker. She went back to the Pontiac. One of the local radio stations had sent a car. The vans from the major networks would be arriving at any moment. Parker remembered the first time she'd been interviewed. She'd watched herself on the eleven o'clock news, and her mother had even made a videotape. But notoriety had a price — half her neighbors weren't talking to her because she refused to fix their parking tickets. And the other half wasn't quite so friendly either, now they knew she was a cop.

Willows finished scouring the lot. He went over to Mel Dutton and said a few words and then walked up and thumped the Pontiac's trunk.

"Had a look inside?"

Parker didn't say anything. She could feel herself blushing. Christ, it could be full of Girl Guides, for all she knew. What a day she was having.

"Not yet," she said.

Willows got a pry bar from the squad car, wedged the thin end of the bar up under the lip of the trunk. He applied force and the bar slipped free. His hand banged into the rear bumper. He swore, sucked a knuckle.

One of the uniforms wandered over. Lambert. All freckles and big white teeth. Lambert had made a name for himself by being the only cop on the force to shoot his own squad car. Maybe that's why he was interested now — because he specialized in automotive mayhem.

"Want a hand?"

Willows gave him the pry bar. Lambert drove the bar home, braced himself, applied downward pressure. The lid popped open. Willows let Lambert get his hands dirty pulling out the spare tire. Underneath the tire there was a jack and a wheel wrench, jumper cables.

"Just like Howard Johnson's," said Lambert.

Willows tilted an eyebrow.

"No surprises," said Lambert. His bright blue eyes admired Parker's legs.

A CKVU TV crew arrived in an Econoline van, began to unload their equipment. "Do me a favor," Willows said to Lambert. "Ask them to get some footage of the crowd."

Lambert trudged across the gravel towards the van.

Willows stared out across the water. It'd be a hell of a place to drag. The guns might be down there, but the victim was probably way out in the harbor somewhere, or the wind and currents might have taken him twenty miles out to sea. Exactly what the city needed, another unsolved crime.

An airhorn sounded and the loose cluster of newspaper reporters, minor television personalities and techs moved aside to let a Buster's towtruck crunch across the gravel in a wide circle, then back slowly towards the Pontiac. When the Ident team was finished with the car, it'd be towed to the police compound for a more leisurely and thorough examination. He made a mental note to give the crime lab a call, see if he could inject some slight sense of urgency into Jerry Goldstein and his team of myopics. He watched the towtruck driver climb out of his cab and then said, "Hungry?"

"Depends who's buying," said Parker.

The towtruck driver had on greasy striped coveralls, a black sleeveless T-shirt and a Yankees baseball cap. He needed a shave. The cigar clenched firmly between his teeth was the same color as the grime impacted beneath his fingernails. "Okay, I admit it, I asked him first," Willows said.

"But he turned you down."

"He already had a date."

"Or he lied."

Willows grinned.

"I wouldn't mind a coffee," said Parker.

On the east side of the parking lot, separated from the road by a chain-link fence, there was a low wooden building about the size of a mobile home, green-stained vertical cedar boards on a concrete pad. Willows led Parker through a gate, down a narrow concrete walkway, past a row of dwarf cedars in wooden barrels, towards a sliding glass door. He pushed open the door and they went inside.

The floor was linoleum, waxed and shiny. Bright green metal tables and bright blue plastic and tubular metal chairs were arranged alongside the window that faced the harbor. Five-gallon aluminum cans were ranged along the windowsill. The cans had once contained German beer or German pickles, but now served as pots for overgrown tomato plants.

Willows scrutinized the menu, which was chalked on a blackboard. A woman approached the table. She was small and tidy, with a pale complexion, the kind of skin that seems to turn powdery with age. She wore her hair in a bun, black shot through with gray. No makeup or jewelry, except for the half-dozen gold wedding and engagement rings that crowded the fingers of her right hand. Willows caught himself looking at the rings and thinking about Mannie Katz, a contract killer with a fatal fondness for jewelry. Willows had shot Katz to death a little more than a year ago, and still hadn't stopped dreaming. He cleared his throat, smiled up at the woman. "Still serving breakfast?"

"All day long."

"I'll have the Special. Eggs easy over."

"Wholewheat toast?"

Willows nodded.

"Coffee?"

"Please."

The woman turned to Parker.

"Just coffee," said Parker. "I'll eat his toast."

"Strawberry jam okay?"

"Perfect."

Outside, a yellow-painted gangway led down to the wooden walkway that started on the far side of the pier. A sign over the gangway advertised the Aquabus, the tiny ferry that made the short run across the water to the shops and farmer's market of Granville Island. Sunlight splintered on the waves. The woman brought coffee, and Willows found himself staring at her rings again, the bands of shining gold, bright spark of diamonds. Mannie Katz leapt out at him from the darkness. His snubbie exploded, the muzzle blast staining Mannie's face pale orange. Mannie's eyes were wide with shock, already glazing.

Willows' hand shook as he dumped a plastic container of cream into his coffee. His spoon rattled against the side of his mug. Parker was staring at him. Their eyes met. Embarrassed, full of wisdom and sympathy, she looked away.

Willows drank some coffee, scorched the roof of his mouth.

The woman brought his breakfast to him on a wide oval plate. The eggs had been done just the way he liked them, and the hashbrowns were home-made. Willows looked at her hand again and this time all he saw was a bunch of rings. No hallucinations. He peppered his eggs — no salt — and started eating. Parker helped herself to his knife. She spread a generous helping of strawberry jam on a slice of toast, chewed vigorously.

Willows had eaten all of his eggs and bacon and most of his potatoes when the woman drifted by with a pot of coffee and a handful of creamers. She had been over by the window, looking out at the parking lot. He said, "Got any idea what's going on over there?"

"No idea at all. Somebody had an accident, I guess." She smiled at Parker. "You two come over on that cute little ferry?"

Parker shook her head, no.

"How late do you stay open?" said Willows.

"We close at four." The woman glanced at her watch, as if for confirmation.

"That's pretty early, isn't it?"

"We're open at eight. I'm here by six-thirty. That's a long enough day for me, mister."

"Do you own the restaurant?"

"Such as it is."

"Are there any other staff?"

"Why, you going to make me an offer?"

Willows smiled. "Was the car there when you closed last night?"

"No, it wasn't."

"You sure about that?"

"Absolutely." She gave Willows a closer look. "You a cop?"

"Was it there when you got to work this morning?"

"Yes."

"You said that was about six-thirty?"

"Twenty past."

Willows checked his watch against the clock on the wall over the doorway leading to the kitchen. "Anybody else around?"

"Not a soul."

"Is anybody living on any of those boats down there?" said Parker.

There was a moment's hesitation. Then the woman said, "Not that I know of." Willows and Parker exchanged a quick look.

"Could I have your name, please," said Willows.

"Edna. Edna Weinberg."

"There was blood in the car," said Parker. Willows frowned at her, but she ignored him. "We think someone was shot," she said. "Maybe murdered."

"Try the *Norwich*," said the woman. "Or *La Paloma*, the big green one down there berthed in the far slip. Don't tell them I sent you."

Willows reached for the last piece of toast. Parker beat him to it.

"Next time," Willows said, "you can buy your own damn breakfast."

Parker licked crumbs from her fingers, grinned. No Girl Guides stuffed in the trunk of the Pontiac. A free meal. Maybe it wasn't going to be such a bad day after all.

6

Alan Paterson was the kind of guy who liked to spend money, buy nice things and look at them and think, that's mine, *I own it*. He was forty-two years old and had lived for the past ten years in a great big rambling house in West Vancouver's prestigious Caulfield Cove area. The house had five bedrooms and two fieldstone fireplaces and four state-of-the-art bathrooms, a kitchen his wife still hadn't entirely figured out. The backyard was mostly solid rock; a gentle waterfall of granite dotted with patches of grass, wild ferns and a handful of evergreens. There was a view of the ocean from almost every room — an ever-changing seascape that didn't stop until it bumped up against the horizon.

Alan's plum-colored sixty-thousand-dollar Porsche Carrera stayed warm and dry in the attached heated garage, next to Lillian's beige thirty-thousand-dollar Turbo Volvo wagon, the one she used to drive their three kids to school in the mornings. There was also a cute little Cal 29 moored down by the Bayshore Hotel, in the city.

Alan hardly ever used the sailboat, but he got a big kick out of talking about it, putting his arm on your shoulder, looking you straight in the eye and telling you he believed it was a sin to live near the water and never go out on it.

He kept a .22 calibre Ruger Mark 2 Bull Barrel on the boat. The gun and a box of ammunition had been given to him several years ago by a businessman from Texas, who hadn't realized or cared that it was illegal to bring a pistol across the border. Alan had shot up a few beer cans, lost interest and more or less forgotten about the weapon.

Until recently.

At the moment, he was thinking about jumping in the Porsche and heading downtown, climbing aboard and using the pistol to blow his stupid brains out.

Paterson owned a computer software company. He had five thousand square feet of downtown office space, a dozen employees, a yearly gross in the neighborhood of six million dollars.

But what he also had was an increasingly competitive market, rising interest rates, an antsy bank manager who was going through a mid-life crisis or maybe just smelled blood. Mortgage and car and personal loan payments that were eating him alive, and several major creditors who suddenly weren't answering the phone.

Six months ago, he'd owned a business that just wouldn't stop growing. Now he was facing almost certain bankruptcy. He still wasn't sure how in hell it had happened.

He turned to look over his shoulder, back up the slope of the deserted beach towards the Porsche. A great little piece of machinery. But his payments were almost a grand a month, and at the moment he was two months in arrears. Any day now, the bank would turn him over to a collection agency, they'd repossess and he'd be almost ten thousand in the hole with nothing to show for it. Worse, they'd wholesale the car to a dealer for maybe thirty thousand and he'd end up riding the bus, stuck with the difference. Another twenty thou in the hole and his credit rating shot all to hell. He jiggled the keys in his hand and thought about tossing them in the ocean and then jumping in after them.

A terrific idea, except he'd already cashed in his insurance policy, so where would Lillian get the money to pay for his funeral?

It was Monday, seven o'clock in the morning. He'd told Lillian he was going to work early, and it was the truth when he'd said it. But then he'd come up against the depressing reality of twenty minutes spent sucking exhaust fumes just to get across the bridge, the crawl through the park and down Georgia Street, the Porsche chugging along at maybe ten miles an hour, tops. And at the end of it all a long day in a dying office. Looking at the traffic, he'd lost heart and decided to take a walk on the beach, clear his mind.

It had been sunny and warm all weekend, but during the night the weather had changed, a cold wind coming in from the west and bringing with it a damp chill, the smell of ocean, dark, lowering clouds and the odd shower. The beach was gray, empty. A depressing landscape. Why the hell had he come down here, anyway?

He'd been sitting on a log near the water's edge. He stood up and went down to the shoreline, watched the waves slap against the stones, fall back, surge forward. The tide was on the rise, almost at its peak. He bent and picked up a stone the size of his fist, threw it as far as he could. There was a white splash and then the water settled and it was impossible to tell where the stone had hit.

He picked up another rock, tossed it in the air and caught it. When he was a kid his father had taught him that there were two kinds of stones, skippers and plunkers. Skippers were smooth and flat, like coins, and when you threw them they bounced across the surface of the water until they lost momentum. Plunkers were what was left over. When you tossed a plunker in the water, that was the sound it made when it hit, *plunk*. All his life he'd thought of himself as a skipper, born to stay afloat. Now it looked as if he was about to sink without a trace.

He turned his back on the plum-colored Porsche and began to walk down the beach, along the tide line, on a course parallel with the water. Even with the sound of the waves on the beach and with his back to the bridge, he could still hear the hum of the traffic, tires on pavement, the roar and throb of engines, every once in a while the screech of a horn.

Distance gave him perspective. He saw tiny little cars full of tiny little people, everybody racing along, blindly confident that today was going to be exactly like yesterday and tomorrow was going to be exactly like today, that life would just go on and on and on.

A wave splashed over his shoe. He danced away from the water's edge, sand and stones grinding under his feet. A gull picked at something half-buried in the sand. As he drew nearer the bird flapped its wings and shuffled away from him, studying him with beady yellow eyes.

He continued to trudge along the beach, tried to focus his mind on his problems, find a way out. He couldn't seem to concentrate, kept drifting away. His beautiful house, his cars. Bang & Olufsen stereo system. Solid oak dining room suite, fridge that gave you cold water and ice cubes when you pushed a button. The education he'd promised himself he'd give the kids. Down the drain, all of it. He owed on everything and he was going to have to kiss it all goodbye. What was going to happen to his family? They depended on him. Christ, the bastards would strip Lillian's Rolex right off her wrist.

Lost in his thoughts, Paterson was almost right on top of the boys before he saw them. There were two of them, one about ten and the other twelve or maybe thirteen. Both wearing sneakers and jeans and identical T-shirts, white with a row of bright orange palm trees. Brothers. The boys were squatting on the sand a few feet from the water and they were so still and quiet that his first thought was to wonder if one of them had been hurt.

Then he saw the gleam of the garbage bag, the ragged hole they'd torn in the shiny plastic and the smaller plastic bag they'd pulled through the hole. The second bag was about the size of an overnighter suitcase. The kids had ripped that bag open as well, and it in turn was full of smaller bags, clear plastic ones filled with a powdery white substance that looked like sugar. They'd opened one of the small bags and the older kid was shaking the powder on to the sand, poking at it with a stick.

The sound of the waves must have covered the crunch of his footsteps, or maybe they were so intent on their game that they simply didn't hear him. He was only a few feet away when the boy with the bag looked up, startled.

Paterson was six feet tall and weighed two hundred and ten pounds. He glared down at the boy, using every inch of his height and every pound of his weight. His heart thumped in his chest. He'd already worked out what he was going to do, and how he was going to do it.

"Police," he said. "What the hell do you kids think you're doing?"

"Nothing."

The smaller kid stood up. The older boy dropped the bag on the sand, wiped white powder from his hands.

"You know what that stuff is?"

"Cocaine?"

"Icing sugar," said Paterson. "Did you taste it?"

The boys shook their heads.

"You know what a stakeout is?"

"Yeah, sure."

"Well that's what this is. A stakeout. And you just fucked it up." He looked at his watch. "Your parents know you're down at the beach all by yourselves?"

The ten year old's face sagged. He looked as if he was about to burst into tears.

"We're supposed to be at the mall," said the older boy.

"I wish you were, kid. Because if you'd done what you were supposed to, you wouldn't have screwed up the stakeout, ruined my whole fucking day." Paterson scooped up the bag full of smaller bags of white powder, slapped it with the flat of his hand to shake the sand from it. He gave the two boys a cold look and started across the beach towards his car.

The bag was heavy, had to weigh at least fifteen or twenty kilos, maybe even more. He wondered what the powder was. Probably the kid was right, it was cocaine.

How could he find out? He'd seen the stuff once, at a party. Walked into the upstairs bathroom and found a couple of secretaries and a guy he knew, a programmer named Ribiero, hunched over a few lines laid out on a magazine on the sink in front of the mirror. Ribiero had looked confused and then smiled and offered him a snort. Alan had said no, and that was that. He'd heard the stuff made you feel terrific and then really down, that it gave you energy and took away twice as much. Also that it was expensive, ripped up your nose and could give you a coronary. So he'd said he thought he'd stick to rye and ginger, thanks anyway.

A jogger wheezed past, a guy in his late twenties wearing baggy shorts and a red sweatshirt, brand-new running shoes. What if it really was a stakeout? The strength drained out of him.

The jogger glanced at him, seemed to slow down, then picked up speed.

Why hadn't he taken Ribiero up on his offer, bent and pinched shut a nostril and sucked up a line, so he'd know what he was doing now? He unlocked the Porsche, got in, tossed the bag on the backseat. He glanced down the beach as he drove out of the parking lot. They were watching him, one of them standing on a log for a better view. He wondered if they'd thought to get his licence number. Doubtful, and anyhow, he was too far away for them to read the plate.

He gave it a little more gas as he turned out of the park, drove past the municipal police station, a queasy feeling building in the pit of his stomach.

The little bastards didn't need to know his licence number. All they had to remember was the plum-colored or mauve or even call it a purple Porsche. West Van was a small community. It would take the cops about an hour to find him, once they started looking.

So what he had to do was get rid of the evidence. Hide it. Put it somewhere safe. The house was out. So was the office. That left his sailboat, the Cal 29 moored down at Coal Harbor.

If the cops did come after him, he'd tell them the kids had been watching too much TV. He hadn't said he was a cop, for one thing. And the powder was a yellowish color, not white, and had been in plastic bottles, not bags. He'd say he'd taken it from them because he thought it might be dangerous, industrial waste, toxic chemicals, something tossed off a freighter. What had he done with it? Dumped it in a municipal litter bin. No, he didn't remember which one.

So what would they be looking at? A solid citizen with one wife, three kids and a dog. And not a doberman or a pit bull, either, but a goddamn dinky little toy poodle who got clipped twice a month at thirty bucks a pop and wore a goddamn rhinestone collar. Jesus, his nose was so clean he could do a Kleenex commercial.

Plus he paid almost five thousand dollars a year in municipal taxes. If that didn't keep them in line, nothing would.

So if the kids did tell mommy about the man on the beach, and mommy bothered to phone the cops and the cops bothered to follow up on it, how hard would they push?

Not very hard at all.

He'd been driving along without thinking about where he was going, reacting automatically to the traffic. Now he found himself on the bridge, heading into the city. He reached behind him and pushed the bag down on the carpeted floor, flattening it and making it harder to see.

On Georgia, he took the first left and drove down towards the harbor, past the Bayshore Hotel. He parked the car, turned off the engine and got out and glanced casually around. There were a few people down by the water, but nobody he knew. He grabbed the bag and wrapped his jacket around it, locked the car, walked rapidly across the lot and down the ramp to the aluminum boathouse that sheltered the Cal 29.

There were a dozen places on board where he could hide the coke, if that's what it was.

He tossed the bag up on the forward deck and grabbed a stanchion and hauled himself aboard. The boat swayed gently on the water. He unlocked the louvered mahogany door. He hadn't taken the boat out since early July. Inside, pale gray light filtered through the small oval windows, and the air smelled musty and damp. He put the garbage bag down on a small folding table. Found an ashtray, lit a cigarette, took the smaller bags out of the bigger one.

There were eighty bags. He used a fish scale to weigh one. Call it half a pound. He found the bag that had a rip in it, licked his finger and tried a taste.

Maybe he wasn't going to turn into a plunker after all.

The younger boy flicked at the sand with his stick. He waited until Paterson had climbed into the Porsche and then said, "That's no cop car."

"It's a Porsche," said his brother. "A Porsche Carrera."

"He sure swore a lot."

"Maybe he was trying to scare us."

"You think he really was a cop?"

"He looked like a cop, didn't he?"

The younger boy nodded. "Yeah, but all adults look like cops, when they're mad." He dug at the sand with his stick. "What if that stuff really was drugs? Maybe we should tell mom about it when she gets home from work."

"We're supposed to be at the mall, remember?"

"How can we be at the mall when it doesn't even open till nine-thirty?"

"If he's really a cop, how come he drives a sports car?"

"All narcs drive expensive cars."

"On TV," said the younger boy.

"What's the difference?" said the twelve year old. But at the same time, he had to admit that maybe his little brother had a point.

7

Inspector Homer Bradley's office was on the third floor of 312 Main. The office was furnished with a large cherrywood desk, one leather chair and two plain wooden ones, a pair of battered three-drawer filing cabinets. The floor was gray linoleum, the walls and ceiling a drab, crab-apple green. The office had only one window. It was small, but afforded a wonderful view over the roof of the adjoining building. On a clear day Bradley could catch a glimpse of the inner harbor, the smoky green bulk of the North Shore mountains.

He finished his brandy-laced coffee, wiped his mouth with a handkerchief and chewed on a breath mint. Nobody had to tell him that drinking on the job was a bad idea. He had a cold, was all. The alcohol helped clear his sinuses. He sniffed the empty mug and detected brandy fumes, slid open a lower drawer and pushed the mug in next to his Smith & Wesson Police Special.

There was a knock on the door, a light tap. He ran his fingers lightly across the barrel and cylinder of the revolver. The metal was cold, clammy. He slammed the drawer shut.

His office door swung open. Parker was wearing a cream-colored blouse and dark green suit, Willows baggy black cords and a black shirt with bright red buttons, black leather Reebok walking shoes. Willows looked as if he'd just told a joke, and Parker looked as if she wasn't quite ready to stop laughing. Bradley popped a breath mint, chewed and swallowed. What the hell was going on, what was so damn funny? Did they know about his cold, his developing penchant for an early morning drink? He put the thought aside. If Willows walked into the office and found him stark naked and dead drunk, he was confident no one would ever hear a word of it.

"Hi, kids." Bradley knocked back another mint, just to be on the safe side. He indicated the wooden chairs ranged along the wall opposite his desk. "Sit down, make yourselves comfy."

Willows remained standing. "You wanted to see us?" he said.

What Willows was doing was reminding Bradley that he was overworked and in a hurry, had no time for idle chat. Bradley was offended, decided to let it show.

"Yeah, I wanted to see you. But then, who wouldn't?" He winked at Parker. "Nice blouse. New?"

Parker nodded, but didn't say anything. She and Willows had been partners a couple of years now; she was starting to pick up his speech patterns.

"Very nice. Have I seen that suit before?"

"I don't think so, Inspector." Parker smiled, gave Bradley the nicest smile he'd had all month.

He reached across the desk for the carved cedar humidor his wife had given to him as a parting gift on the day their divorce had been finalized. Hadn't she realized that half the pleasure he got from smoking came from her constant nagging at him to stop? He flipped open the lid and chose a cigar, clipped the end and lit up with a big wooden kitchen match.

Willows, reformed smoker, stared up at the ceiling.

"Must've cost a bundle," said Bradley. He waited a moment and when Parker didn't respond, raised an eyebrow and leaned towards her across the polished surface of his desk. "Your beautiful new suit," he explained.

"It was a present."

"No kidding."

"My mother gave it to me."

Bradley blew a stream of smoke towards the scaly, leprous ceiling. The smoke swirled and twisted around the buzzing fluorescent lights; the room seemed to darken. He chewed on the cigar for a moment and then said, "What was the occasion, you don't mind me asking?"

"My birthday."

Willows, Bradley noted with satisfaction, actually seemed to flinch with amazement.

"Your birthday! Isn't that wonderful!" Chuckling merrily,

Bradley slid open the bottom drawer of his desk and pulled out a paper plate containing three muffins gaily decorated with white and green icing, each muffin sporting a single candle. He struck a match, lit the candles, and started to sing 'Happy Birthday'. When Willows didn't join in, Bradley glared at him until he did.

"Make a wish!" said Bradley.

Parker puffed her cheeks and blew out the candles. She helped herself to a muffin. Bradley broke open a six-pack of cold Coke, handed out paper napkins decorated with cartoon dragons. "So how does it feel, the big three-zero?"

"Terrible."

"Maybe this'll help." Bradley handed Parker a small rectangular box wrapped in glossy chocolate-brown paper and topped off with a thin gold ribbon, complicated bow. Parker turned a lovely shade of pink.

"Your age," said Bradley, "and still blushing like a baby."

Parker fumbled with the ribbon, managed to slip the knot. She crumpled the glossy paper into a ball, tossed it overhand into Bradley's wastebasket. She held the Birks blue box in both hands, smiled at Bradley, "What is it?"

"And you claim to be a detective." Bradley flicked ash at the wastebasket, missed by an inch.

Parker opened the box. Lying on a bed of white tissue was a pair of earrings in the form of tiny roses; petals of gold, ruby flowers.

"They're lovely."

"My pleasure."

"Whenever I wear them, I'll think of you."

Now it was Bradley's turn to blush. He puffed furiously on his cigar, laying down a smokescreen. "The car under the bridge. Got anything yet?"

Willows swallowed the last of his muffin, drank some Coke. "What we've got is a problem, Inspector. What we don't have is a body."

"But there's one out there somewhere, let's hope."

"We have evidence of a shooting," said Parker. "It looks like the victim was shot by someone who was sitting beside him in the front seat, then shot again two or more times from directly behind. So at least two guns were used, both of them automatics."

Bradley nodded, brushed muffin crumbs from his lap.

"We found three spent casings in the car," Willows said. "Primary indications from forensics, firing pin and extractor marks on the shell casing, indicate that the big gun was a Colt, the twenty-five a Star."

"We also have a quantity of blood," said Parker. "A classic splash pattern, bone fragments and brain tissue. The ME is of the opinion that the bone fragments came from a human skull and that the large quantity of tissue recovered from the crime scene would have resulted in the instantaneous death of the victim."

"Whose name is?"

"Unknown," said Parker.

"At the moment," amended Willows.

Bradley pulled on his cigar, emitted a billowing noxious cloud, sighed with pleasure. "Fingerprints?"

"Nothing. The car had been wiped clean."

"So you're telling me somebody was shot to death, but you don't know who. You have no victim and you have no suspects."

"We are the police," said Willows. "We are trained to suspect everyone."

Bradley rolled his eyes. "Gimme a break, Jack. Was there any sign of a struggle? Did the shooting actually take place under the bridge, at the crime scene? Or did the victim get splashed somewhere else?"

"The car wasn't driveable. The windshield was smashed all to hell and there were splinters of glass on the ground beside the car. There was a struggle, all right. I'd say the shoot took place where we found the car."

"Got a time frame?"

"We checked the neighborhood, such as it is," said Parker. "There isn't much down there. A new condo, a few small businesses and a construction site. The car wasn't there at ten o'clock Friday night. Nobody we've talked to noticed it at all, on Saturday, except for Mrs Weinberg."

"Who?"

"She owns a restaurant down by the dock. The perfect witness. Bright. Articulate. An eye for detail. Only problem is, she didn't see anything."

"Naturally. Anything else?"

"Two things," said Willows. "There's an Aquabus wharf down there in sight of the parking lot, and the kid who was piloting the Sunday morning run quit work at the end of his shift. Didn't give any notice, just took off. We've got an address but no phone number."

"You think he saw something?"

"Could be. We'll let you know."

"Next?"

"Under the bridge, there was an abandoned car. An Oldsmobile, a Cutlass. No plates, a flat tire, the whole thing covered in bird shit. In the back seat there was an old sleeping bag, newspapers . . ."

"You figure somebody's using the car to coop?"

Willows nodded.

"The missing kid, the Cutlass. Who's on it?"

"We are."

"You and your rapidly aging partner."

Willows nodded.

"Get somebody else," said Bradley. He shuffled some papers on his desk. "Take Farley Spears."

"He's got the flu. His wife said he'd probably be gone for the week."

Bradley studied his cigar. He'd made a secret pact with himself that in the interest of his continued good health he would no longer smoke his cigars closer than three inches to the butt, and that's just about what he was down to. He reached for the ashtray and then thought better of it and stuck the cigar in his mouth and sucked in one last puff. "What about Eddy Orwell?"

"What about him?"

"Come on, Jack. All he has to do is knock on a few doors, ask a few questions."

"And remember the answers."

Smoke dribbled out of Bradley's nostrils. "What's next?"

"We're gonna take another run at the neighborhood, knock on a few doors. See if we can get lucky."

"Gonna drag the creek?"

"At slack tide, three o'clock this afternoon."

"You've got a full plate, Jack, no two ways about it. Orwell gets a shot at the kid."

Willows started towards the door.

"What did you think of the muffin?" said Bradley.

Willows paused with his hand on the knob, giving it some thought. "Moist," he said at last. "Fluffy."

"Betty Crocker," said Bradley. "Just follow the directions, you can't go wrong."

Willows had found a wooden crate and dragged it over to the huge concrete column, had his penknife out and was digging away at something about ten feet above ground level. High above him, the unseen flock of starlings twittered excitedly.

"What've you got?" said Parker.

"Lead scrapings. Probably from the bullet that went through the windshield."

Willows finished getting his scrapings and then said something Parker didn't catch, and wandered over to the construction site. Parker waited until he was out of sight and then stood on the packing crate and studied the fresh scar in the cement. After a moment she climbed down from the crate and went over to the Cutlass, got a Kleenex out of her purse and opened the door. Several oddly-shaped pieces of blue foam-board — insulation stolen from the nearby job site — had been wedged up against the windows and placed under a raggedy sleeping bag. So Willows was right, someone was sleeping in the car.

Parker wondered what kind of hours he kept, if he'd been home on Friday night, had heard or seen anything that might further the investigation.

She heard footsteps on the gravel, turned and saw Willows walking towards her. She slammed shut the Cutlass' door, indicated the construction site. "Any luck?"

Willows shook his head. "I thought the foreman or someone

from one of the sub-trades might have decided to work through the weekend. Not a chance."

Parker indicated the lead smear. "I should've seen that yesterday."

Willows shrugged. "The light was different." He put his foot up on the bumper of the Cutlass. "Anybody home?"

"Not at the moment."

Willows wasn't surprised. The vagrant would be gone at first light, back after dark. Careful because he knew that if anybody from the condo or one of the businesses happened to see him, they'd have the car towed away. He glanced at his watch. "Might as well get to work on the condo."

"Okay," said Parker.

The condominium was nine storeys high, built of prefab concrete slabs, with a sloped roof of corrugated sheet steel painted aquamarine. At the front of the building, glass-enclosed balconies looked out over the water. Willows had gauged the angle and decided the balconies would have an unobstructed view of the lower half of the parking lot.

There were eighteen apartments in the condo; two per floor. Willows buzzed the super, and they were let into the lobby.

The super was tall, balding. He had a heavy frame and thick, sloping shoulders, an Eastern European accent.

"Who you want to see this time?" He spoke to Willows, ignored Parker.

Willows turned to Parker.

"The people we didn't see yesterday," she said.

"Mrs Livingston not home. She saw nothing. She is sorry, but cannot help you."

"We'll try her again tomorrow," Parker said. "Or in the evening, if that's more convenient."

"She saw nothing," the super said to Willows. "She watch TV, go to bed early."

"That's what she told you," said Parker. "But is it what she'd tell us?"

The ground floor of the condo contained the super's apartment, storage areas, a spacious and well-furnished lobby. Willows and Parker had already questioned the occupants of the second and third floors. He went over to the elevator and pushed the UP button. The doors immediately slid open. They stepped inside. The super made as if to follow them.

"Wait there," said Parker.

The super opened his mouth. The doors slid shut.

The owner of apartment 437 was Miss Susan Tyler. Miss Tyler was waiting for them at the door when they came out of the elevator. She was wearing a mauve pleated skirt and a white blouse, fleecy wool slippers. Her hair was cut short, and was silvery gray except for a feathering of mauve at her temple on the left side. She wore a heavy gold necklace and wedding and engagement rings, large gold hoops that pulled at her earlobes, a gold chain around her ankle.

"How old would you say I am?" was her opening remark.

Willows turned to Parker, raised an eyebrow.

"I'm speaking to you, young man."

"Detective Willows. And this is Detective Parker. We're investigating a shooting and possible homicide that took place Friday night in the parking lot under the Granville Street bridge."

"Yes, I'm aware of that. Terrible, simply terrible. George told me all about it. You don't look surprised. Well, neither would I. The man's a bit of a gossip, I wouldn't share any of *my* secrets with him."

Willows nodded politely. George was the super.

Susan Tyler opened her door a little wider. The gold jangled. "Why don't you come inside, so we can sit down and be comfortable."

There was a spacious entrance hall, mirrored closet doors on the left and to the right a wide hallway that Willows guessed led to the bedrooms. The apartment was fairly large — George had told Willows and Parker that except for the penthouse, each unit had two bedrooms and a den, and occupied a little over three thousand square feet.

The two detectives followed Miss Tyler across an expanse of white plush carpet and into the living room. Willows had expected antiques, but the furniture was modern and comfortable, expensive but understated. Parker went over to the sliding glass doors that led to the balcony, paused with her hand on the latch.

"Go ahead, dear. Make yourself at home."

Parker slid open the door and stepped out on the balcony.

Miss Tyler waved Willows towards the couch, sat down beside him. "Now then," she said, "where were we?"

"We were about to discuss the shooting in the parking lot," said Willows.

"No we weren't, not quite yet." She moved closer to Willows and patted him on the arm. Her nails, long and sharp and painted jet black, hissed across the fabric of his jacket. "Since you're a detective, you must be very good at guessing people's ages. In fact I imagine it's part of your training. So tell me, please, how old would you say I am?"

"Sixty-seven," said Willows.

"That's a very clever guess, young man. Close enough to seem sincere, but far enough off to be flattering. As a matter of fact I'm seventy-two."

"Amazing," said Willows. He smiled. "Did you hear the shots?"

"No, I'm afraid not."

"Did you see anything? The lights of a car, people down by the water . . ."

"No, I'm sorry. Not a thing. As soon as it gets dark I pull the curtains. The windows are double-glazed, and the curtains are very thick and help contain the noise from the bridge. The sound of traffic can be very loud, you know. And of course I don't like the idea of people looking in on me, invading my privacy."

The balcony door slid open and Parker came back into the room. She closed the door and briskly rubbed her hands together.

"Cold, isn't it?" said Miss Tyler. "It's the wind off the water that does it. My husband bought this place about six months before he died, and I really wish he hadn't, bless his soul. It's lovely in the summer, but during the rest of the year it's cold and damp, not much fun at all. And the balcony's useless, because of the traffic noise from the bridge."

Willows stood up. He took a card from his wallet.

"Won't you stay and have a cup of tea?" said Miss Tyler. "Or I have coffee, if you prefer."

"We'd love to," said Parker, "but we're really very busy."

"I was out this morning and bought some muffins. Bran muffins, with raisins. They're nice and fresh, I could pop them in the microwave and they'd be ready in less than a minute."

"Coffee and a muffin would be perfect," said Willows, avoiding Parker's eye.

"Well then, you two just make yourselves comfortable and I'll put the kettle on."

Parker sat in a wing-back chair on the far side of the room, over by the television.

"What're you looking at me like that for?" Willows whispered across the room. He grinned. "It's twenty to two. Just because you've had your lunch doesn't mean I can't have mine."

In the kitchen a coffee grinder whined shrilly, drowning Parker's earthy response.

They left the condo at ten minutes past three. The owners had been home at five of the sixteen apartments they'd visited. They'd interviewed seven of the owners on the previous day, Sunday afternoon. Twelve down and four to go, but Willows was confident they weren't going to come up with anything, because why would anybody in his right mind spend a perfectly nice Saturday evening staring out the window at an unlit parking lot?

Maybe Eddy Orwell would get lucky. Or maybe the bum who was living in the Cutlass had seen something.

Anything was possible, wasn't it?

The first diver hit the water at twenty minutes past three. The last diver came out of the water at five minutes past six. He had something on the end of a yellow nylon rope. Willows and Parker, huddled on shore, watched as the stiff coils of rope piled up on the deck of the Coast Guard cruiser.

The water bulged, frothed white. It took Willows a moment to realize that the shiny black object on the end of the rope was an old tire. It was a few more moments before he identified the manic sound floating across the water towards him as laughter.

Willows saluted the diver with a stiff middle finger. Then turned to glance behind him, and was relieved to see Miss Tyler wasn't at her window, to observe his childish and petulant behavior.

8

The client was a sushi freak. Paterson had arranged to meet him for lunch at one o'clock sharp at a trendy Japanese restaurant on Burrard. He'd reserved a private room. The room was about ten feet square, with authentic paper walls, a hardwood floor, and a low table with a pit beneath it so stiff-legged Westerners could hunker down and dine in comfort.

The food was attractively presented and very tasty, but Paterson was so distracted by his thoughts that he hardly knew what he was eating. The client, his mouth full of Kirin beer and raw fish and bright ideas, spoke with such great energy and enthusiasm that he failed to notice Paterson hardly heard a word he said.

That morning, Paterson had looked up his pal Jerry Ribiero, the programmer with the thirsty nose. He showed Ribiero a baggie containing a soupspoon of the white powder, asked him to confirm that the powder was cocaine.

Ribiero had picked the bag up off his desk, hefted the weight of it and held it up against the blue-tinted light flooding in from the plate-glass windows of his office. "You wired, Al?"

"What?"

"Wearing a wire. Electronic listening device, know what I mean?"

"Jesus, Jerry!"

"Look me in the eye, Al. Narcs gotcha by the balls? You workin' for the narcs?"

"Do I look like a narc, Jerry?"

"Yeah, as a matter of fact, you do. But so does everybody else, ain't life a bitch." Ribiero tore open a pack of cigarettes, flicked a green plastic disposable lighter. "Where'd you get it, Al?"

"I found it."

"Lucky you." Ribiero nervously flicked the lighter, cupped his hand around the flame.

"One of my kid's school pals had it on him. Kid slung his jacket over the banister and the bag fell out of his pocket. Simple as that."

Ribiero grinned, kept flicking his Bic. "So you told him you were gonna have to confiscate the stuff, right?"

"I didn't say anything. When they went upstairs to Jamie's room, I put the bag in my pocket."

"At today's prices, who could blame you?"

"I'm not going to snort it, Jerry. I just want to confirm that it's coke."

The programmer fiddled with the bag, unfastening the tie-tab. "You're saying you don't want it? That once you have my professional opinion, it's all mine?"

"Why not?"

"You should be wearing a fluffy white beard, Al, and big black boots and a red velvet suit." The knot came loose. "You got at least fifteen or twenty grams here, the kid must be a dealer. If I were you, I'd make your boy piss in a bottle, run a urinalysis on him."

"He's okay."

"Hey, sure. Whatever you say." Ribiero licked his finger, dipped it in the white powder. Frowned.

"Something wrong?"

"It's too fine, not gritty enough. Like somebody's already chopped it." Ribiero lifted his finger to his nose, sniffed. Licked. Gave Al a look.

"What?" said Paterson.

"This isn't coke, it's fucking heroin."

"Heroin?"

"Smack. H. White lady. Junk. Call it whatever you want, it still bottoms out at about five years' worth of hard time."

Paterson couldn't think of anything to say. "Are you sure, Jerry?"

"I tried it once. Back in the sixties. Remember the sixties, Al? Jesus, in those days I was doing every damn thing there was. Had a big glass milk bottle full of pills in the refrigerator. Peyote . . . A friend of mine was a dealer. Ross Venturino. He was mostly into weed, but he did special orders. His wholesaler gave him a couple of hits, a freebie. We passed the stuff around. I had a taste. Ross was a little crazier. He shot up, mainlined. Drilled himself right in that big vein runs through the crook of your elbow. Said it was the best experience of his life. Better than sex. When he came down, he took the second hit and flushed it right down the toilet."

Ribiero sealed the plastic bag and pushed it across the table. "The drug itself can't hurt you, if it's pure. Unless you get unlucky and overdose. But once you're wired, odds are you're gonna die one way or the other, sooner or later. Starve yourself to death because you'd rather feed your veins than eat. Fall out of a window trying to break into somebody's apartment. Get cut up by another junkie. Share a needle and cop hepatitis, or maybe AIDS. Pop a hot shot. Nod off smoking and burn to death."

"What's a hot shot?" said Paterson.

"Shooting up with smack that hasn't been stepped on, diluted. When you're wired, Al, there's a million ways to go."

Paterson picked up the bag and put it away in his coat pocket.

"Talk to your kid, Al. In fact, if it was me, I'd call the cops."

"Thanks for your help, Jerry."

Paterson winced as a hand fell on his shoulder. He twisted and glanced behind him and saw that it was only the waitress. She saw the look in his eyes and shuffled backwards, putting distance between them.

"She wants to know if there's something wrong with the food," said the client.

Al shook his head. "No, it's fine. I just got carried away by what you were saying."

The client smiled.

Paterson picked up his glass, drank some beer. It tasted warm and flat. He snuck a peek at his watch. Quarter past two. The client had done all the talking, but it was his plate that was empty, Paterson's that was full.

"Would you like anything more to drink?" said the girl.

"Uh . . ."

"I wouldn't mind another beer," said the client.

"Make it two," said Paterson automatically. Then his brain clicked in and he added, "And could you bring me the bill, please."

"Busy afternoon?"

Paterson ignored the hint of reproof in the client's voice. "Booked solid. Christ, I keep thinking we're as busy as we're ever going to get, and we just keep getting busier."

It was almost three by the time he got back to the office, and by then he'd made up his mind exactly what he was going to do.

He had his secretary, Kathy, get Lillian on the phone. His wife told him a registered letter from the bank had come in the mail, asked him should she open it. He told her not to touch the damn thing, crossed his fingers and told her a lie, that something had come up and he was on his way to the airport, was flying to Toronto and wouldn't be back for at least three days.

Kathy must have been listening through the open door, because when he came out of his office she asked him if he wanted her to call a cab.

"I'll take the Porsche."

"You're going to leave your beautiful new car all alone in an uncovered parking lot for three whole days?"

"My flight leaves in less than an hour, Kathy. I haven't got time to wait for a cab."

"What about car thieves? Vandalism?" Kathy smiled at him with her mouth and eyes. "My God, what if it rains?"

Paterson shrugged into his coat and grabbed his briefcase.

"Have fun!" Kathy called after him as he hurried out the door.

Paterson drove the Porsche to the nearest branch of his bank and used his Visa card to obtain a cash advance of one thousand dollars.

From the bank he drove down to Coal Harbor and retrieved a half-pound bag of heroin and his Ruger and fifty rounds of hollowpoints from the Cal 29. The gun was still in the original box, coated in a thin layer of oil to protect it from the salt air. The weapon felt cold and sticky in his hands. He ejected the magazine and filled it with ten LR hollowpoints. Now that the pistol was loaded it was much heavier. He extended his right arm, locked his elbow and aimed at the porthole above the galley stove. The porthole was about the size of a man's head. Paterson tried to imagine pulling the trigger, shooting someone. Impossible. So what in hell was the point of taking the gun? He put it back in the box and then, not knowing why he was doing it, put the box in his briefcase. On his way out, he used a penknife to scratch the varnished mahogany around the door lock, making it look as if someone had tried a break and enter.

The wharfinger wasn't in his office. Paterson wrote a short note in which he said it appeared as if someone had tried to break into his boat, asked the wharfinger to keep an eye on the vessel. He folded the note in half and wedged it under the dial of the wharfinger's phone.

He walked back to the car, stowed the Ruger and fifty rounds of ammunition in the trunk, and drove to the part of the city known as Gastown.

Gastown was located to the north of the downtown core, pressed up against the network of railway tracks that parallels the waterfront. It is one of Vancouver's oldest areas, and was named after 'Gassy Jack', a riverboat captain and accomplished drinker who opened Gastown's first retail business, the Globe Saloon. During the Depression, Gastown began its decline. By the sixties it was one of the worst skid rows in the country. In the mid-seventies, the city developed a plan to revitalize the area — cobble the streets and sidewalks, sandblast the old brick buildings, install atmospheric lighting — build a better tourist trap.

Paterson parked his Porsche in the Woodwards parking lot. He locked the car and triggered the alarm system, then took the elevator down to street level, walked over to Hastings Street and east along Hastings until he found the kind of hotel he was looking for.

The Vance advertised rooms by the day or month. A battered wooden door opened on a steep, dimly-lit flight of stairs. There was no lobby. Paterson walked slowly up the stairs. At the landing there was a wire-mesh door. The door was locked. He banged on it with the flat of his hand, making the mesh rattle. Someone yelled at him to shut up. He yelled back that he wanted a room.

There was the sound of a buzzer. The door clicked off the latch.

He pushed the door open and let it swing shut behind him. To his left there was a long hallway and another flight of stairs, to the right a small wired-in cubicle, and beyond the cubicle another hallway. Squinting in the glare of the lights, he walked over to the cubicle and looked inside. A man sitting in a plain wooden chair stared back at him. The man was in his late twenties, thin almost to the point of emaciation, wearing a vest of black leather, no shirt, faded jeans. He had a pale, narrow face and small, dark eyes. His hair was glossy black, combed straight back from a high forehead. He needed a shave. A tiny diamond sparkled in his left ear. He reached up to run his fingers through his hair and Paterson saw that his nails were painted pale blue and had been filed to a sharp point.

The man waggled a finger. "Got a search warrant, honey?"

"No, but I've got twenty bucks."

The man stood up. He rested his bony elbows on the counter and leaned forward, his eyes bright and mocking.

"Saying you ain't a cop, pretty face?"

Paterson could smell the man's perfume, his hair oil, after-shave, the scent of his deodorant. And lurking beneath the surface, the stench of his unwashed body.

Paterson laid a twenty on the counter. "Got a room, sport?"

The man eyed Paterson's tie, his button-down shirt, the five-hundred-dollar suit. He got up on his toes and pressed against the edge of the counter, gasped in mock admiration at the crease in Paterson's pants, the shine on his shoes. He stared unblinkingly into Paterson's eyes, weighing and measuring him, clearly finding him wanting. Finally he shrugged and said, "The room's ten bucks a night. Twenty'll buy you two nights. There's a five-dollar deposit on the key."

"Fine," said Paterson.

"Sign the register."

Paterson wrote Jerry Ribiero's name in an illegible scrawl. The twenty disappeared. A room key was slapped down on the counter.

"You go out, leave the key with me or whoever's at the desk.

You ain't allowed to take it outta the hotel, unnerstand? And remember, you lose it you can kiss your deposit goodbye."

The number on the key was 318.

The man jerked a thumb over his shoulder, glossy blue nails gleaming in the light. "Room's down at the far end of the hall. No loud noises or music or company after ten o'clock. No alcohol or drugs. Bend the rules and we'll kick your ass out on the street."

Paterson scooped up the key and started to walk away from the desk. He stopped, turned. "Can you get me a woman?"

"Do I *procure*, you mean?"

"Yeah, that's right."

"Lemme see your wallet. Flip it open for me, let's see you got a badge."

Paterson flipped open his wallet. It was alligator, a little thicker than a credit card.

"How many you want, sport?"

"Three."

"Yeah? Really? Ambitious, eh? How long you gonna need 'em? Couple minutes? An hour? The rest of your life?"

"An hour, probably less."

"Cost you sixty apiece." He glanced at Paterson's briefcase. "More, if you're into whipped cream or whips, shit like that."

"Fifty," said Paterson with as much firmness and conviction as he could muster.

The man nibbled his lip, grunted. "I got no idea what game you're playing, sweetie. But about half an hour from now, you gonna have all the players you need to make a team."

Room 318 had a floor of cracked green linoleum. The walls were painted a muddy yellow. A naked low-wattage bulb hung from the ceiling. The only furniture in the room was a narrow bed and a dusty bureau. A cracked sink occupied the corner diagonally opposite the room's sole window. The window had a terrific view of the alley, a trio of dumpsters overflowing with rotting garbage.

Paterson took the Ruger out of his briefcase. He checked the safety, put the gun in his trenchcoat pocket and sat down on the bed.

Now all he had to do was wait.

9

Gary Silk was stretched out on the burgundy leather couch in the den, watching baseball on his big Sony TV, his head cradled in Samantha's lap. Samantha was twenty years old, a Capricorn, born on December twenty-third. Gary had said it must be a bitch, having a birthday so close to Christmas. Samantha had given him a big smile, letting him know she considered him a pretty insightful guy.

Encouraged, he'd asked her when she got off work and she'd said, "How about right this minute," stripped off her apron and told him not to move, she was just going in the back to get her purse.

Quit her job for him, just like that.

She'd been on the wrong side of the Orange Julius counter at Oakridge, a big shopping mall up by Queen Elizabeth Park. She'd been kind of young for Gary's taste; as a general rule he liked his women a bit older, because while age didn't necessarily bring wisdom, it did tend to wear off the sharp edges, make the ladies a little less volatile, more likely to stay in line, do what they were told.

But youth had its compensations, there was no doubt about that.

One thing Gary liked about Samantha was that she was a real sports fan, liked to lick the salt from the rim of her margarita glass and watch those big black boys get up to the plate, adjust the crotch, take a practice swing with the bat. Gary had been kidding her about it all night long, pretending the sexy things she said pissed him off. But the truth was that the way she talked, the tone of voice and words she used, really turned him on, got the blood churning and galloping through his veins.

Gary smiled into his drink. They wouldn't have let her use those words back at the Orange Julius counter, that's for sure. He reached out and ran his fingers down the long curving length of her, through her silky blonde shoulder-length hair and across her breast and hip, the smoothness of her thigh. He had a plan. At about the fifth or maybe sixth inning he was going to pick her up and take her down the hall into the bedroom. By then she'd have knocked off, the way she was going, at least three margaritas. Be interesting to see if she could remember what he liked when she was stone drunk. They happened to miss the rest of the game, Frank would tape it. He'd done it before.

The Blue Jays were playing the California Angels. Gary watched Jesse Barfield wait on a slider that was low and away, lean out over the plate and drive the ball high into the lights, over the fence and into the right field stands, thirty rows up. Two runs scored. It was top of the second, nobody out. The Jays were already leading three to zip, pounding those Angels into the dust.

Gary ran his hand across Samantha's hip, his mind on the route he'd jogged that morning, Frank trailing along behind in the Mercedes, a Mozart piano concerto pounding out of the speakers because Frank didn't know how to work Gary's new Compact Disc player and was afraid to mess with it because he might break something.

Gary never had breakfast, but he thought about what he'd eaten for lunch and exactly how much time he'd spent playing squash with the pro that afternoon, and what he'd had for dinner that night. When he'd finished calculating, calories in and calories out, he gave Samantha a squeeze and told her to get her ass over to the bar, fetch him a nice cold bottle of Molson Lite.

"Want one, Frank, while she's up?"

"Yeah, thanks."

Samantha brought the bottles over to Gary and he screwed off the caps and threw them in the gas fireplace. He pointed at Frank and she crossed the room and handed him a beer.

"Thanks, Gary," said Frank.

Gary said, "My pleasure, Frank." He patted the couch. Samantha looked at him. Gary drank some beer. She sat down next to him and he put his arm around her and tilted her head up, kissed her. She finished off the first margarita of the night. There were a few grains of coarse salt on her upper lip. He stuck out his tongue and licked the salt off her and she said, "That's gross!" pushed him away and made him laugh so hard he almost spilled his beer.

He moved back, ran his hand over her. Watched the Jays score another run on a pair of singles and a sacrifice fly. He slipped his hand under her skirt. "Good game, Frank."

Frank didn't say anything. He was staring fixedly at the screen, the untouched bottle of beer cradled in his lap. Gary had a feeling he was a million miles away. Frank was some fucking bodyguard. Gary wondered what he could be thinking, that was fascinating enough to take his mind off the game.

Frank was thinking about Friday night. He was thinking about Oscar Peel, and Pat Nash.

Frank had made Nash drive the Pontiac all the way downtown and under the bridge, Oscar sitting up front next to Nash, in the passenger seat. He'd thought about sticking Oscar in the trunk, but that seemed like kind of a dumb idea; something Tony Curtis would do in a gangster movie, Marilyn Monroe wriggling and squealing in the background.

Frank snuck a quick, contemptuous look at the dumb blonde from the Orange Julius stand. No doubt about it, Gary could really pick 'em. When it came to women, he was about as predictable as a fart in a beanery.

The ride downtown hadn't been too bad, except Nash was too nervous to think straight. Frank had to keep reminding him to speed up or slow down, not bother stopping when the light was green.

Traffic stuff, nothing serious. Nothing to worry about, yet.

Frank had killed before. He knew that a failure of imagination rarely failed to occur; that for most people death was never real until the event was actually about to happen. But at the last moment, and Frank didn't have any idea why this happened, the victims always went one of only two ways. What they did was almost fall asleep on you, or go completely berserk.

So when they turned off Beach and went down Granville towards the water, Frank got ready.

The lights of the car shone on the roundabout. Nash slowed the car and Frank had to tell him to go left. The road was gravel. They hit a pothole, bucked and swayed. Frank almost squeezed the trigger right there, but a part of his brain told him that Nash wasn't trying to get cute, it was just the Pontiac needed new shocks.

The road turned right. On their left there was a chain-link fence, empty space, the outline of a few boats and a low, dark building. No lights except down on the water, where there was a narrow wharf and maybe a couple of dozen sailboats. Frank wondered if anybody lived on them. The water gleamed darkly. He leaned across the seat and pointed. "Over there, Pat."

Nash started into the turn and Oscar leaned over, grabbed the wheel, got his boot in and stomped on the gas pedal. The rear wheels spat gravel and the Pontiac shot towards the harbor.

Frank grabbed at the steering wheel. Oscar tried to stick his fist in his eye. The goddamn car was still accelerating. Oscar had apparently decided that if *he* was going to die, *everybody* was going to die. Frank went for the ignition keys, intending to turn the engine off. Oscar bit him in the neck.

Frank stopped thinking and started reacting. He cocked the .45 and tried to shoot Oscar in the back of the head. The muzzle blast lit up the interior of the car. The sound of the shot was deafening.

Oscar's cheeks bulged. Pink foam sprayed out of his wide-flared nostrils. Frank'd missed at a range of maybe six inches. The windshield was frosted over. Oscar had a hand on the Colt, was trying to take it away from him. Frank jerked back, put a bullet through the roof. Oscar clawed wildly at his face. Frank batted away his hands and tried to line up another shot.

The Pontiac slowed abruptly, the nose dropping. Pat Nash had stuck out his foot and hit the brakes. Bless you, thought Frank. A fraction of a second later the car smashed into a concrete pillar, one of the bridge pilings. Frank was lifted out of his seat. His head hit a side window. Glass shattered. He fell back on the seat. Somebody was screaming. The voice sounded vaguely familiar. The car veered sideways and stopped at an odd angle, nose up, the front end sticking out over the water, the left headlight lighting a pathway to heaven. Frank caught a glimpse of himself in the rearview mirror, shut his mouth.

The screaming stopped.

There was blood all down the front of Oscar Peel's face but he was alive, conscious, desperately trying to force his way out of the car but too panicked to think of opening the door first.

"Do it," said Frank. He handed Pat Nash the dinky little .25 calibre Star, thrusting it into his open hand and at the same time keeping the Colt on him. Nash gave Frank a look Frank had never seen before, rage and grief and a kind of empty hopelessness. He twisted in his seat and put the muzzle of the Star against Oscar's ear.

Oscar jerked his head sideways. His hands tore at the tape that sealed his mouth shut.

Pat Nash had an idea, just like that. He jammed the stubby barrel of the Star up against Oscar's plump hip. Oscar punched him in the mouth. The gun went off. Oscar started bouncing up and down like he'd sat on the world's biggest tack. Nash couldn't say whether or not Oscar'd been hit. Oscar was banging his shoulder against the car door but it wouldn't open.

"Stay still, dammit!" Frank was trying to get set, but Oscar wouldn't stop squirming and wriggling, and it was dark, and it wasn't going to be easy. Frank lunged at him, came away with a fistful of hair. There was something in Oscar's hand, the glint of metal. The door handle. Oscar got down on the floor of the car and did his best to hide under the brake pedal. Frank gritted his teeth and shot him in the ass. What a life. Oscar burrowed deeper. Frank reached down, grabbed Oscar's jeans, tried to haul him upright. There was a movement to his right. Nash hit him on the ear with the Star. Suddenly Frank was in Vegas — there were flashing colored lights all over the place. He grunted, shook his head. His vision cleared. He swung the Colt and Nash went down. Frank's heart was pounding hard enough to break his ribs, his throat was on fire and he could hardly breathe. He got a bead on Oscar Peel, shot him once and then shot him again, shot him a third time and saw in the bright orange lightning bolt of the muzzle flash that the last two rounds had been wasted, Oscar was down for the count.

Nash groaned. Frank pushed him out of the way and opened the passenger-side rear door of the car. He got out and looked around. Nothing. He opened the front door and dragged Oscar's body across the seat. Nash fell half out of the car. His head hit the gravel.

Frank got Oscar all the way out of the car and let him drop. He went around to the far side of the car and peered down at the water. There was a kind of backwater down by the pier. No current, that he could see. Not a good place to put Oscar. He walked backwards diagonally across the parking lot, past a birdshit-splattered Cutlass, to the water's edge. Almost directly below him, five or six feet down, there was a narrow wharf, a floating walkway. He jumped lightly down, grabbed Oscar by the lapels and pulled him on to the dock and dragged him out as close to the main current as he could get. There was a smear of blood on the boards. Well, so what?

Frank pulled Oscar upright, gave him a push. Oscar looked as if he was learning to dive and had no talent. His body collapsed into the water. A headstone of froth, then nothing. Frank stepped on something, glanced down. Oscar's wallet lay on the boards. He took the cash and tossed the wallet into the water. Looked for Oscar, but couldn't find him, despite the bright yellow rain slicker, which he should've taken off, so the body'd be harder to spot in the water. He could feel blood on his hands, sticky and warm. He crouched and washed himself off, rinsed his face. Salt stung his eyes.

When Frank got back to the car, Pat Nash was sitting on the back bumper with his head in his hands, as if he had a flat tire and was waiting for someone to come along and fix it for him.

"Where's the gun?" said Frank.

Nash showed him the Star.

"Get rid of it." Frank jerked his head towards the water.

Nash pushed himself upright, staggered like a drunk across the gravel, fell down. Frank started towards him. Nash stood up. He took a few more steps and made an overhand throwing motion. Frank heard a distant splash.

He started wiping down the car, using a rag he'd brought along for the job, methodically obliterating any and all fingerprints.

"Want some help?"

Frank shook his head. Something his daddy had taught him: you need something done good, better do it yourself. He finished wiping down the car and jammed the rag in his back pocket and started walking up the road towards Beach Avenue.

"Where the hell you going?" said Nash. His voice sounded thin, shaky.

"Get a drink," Frank said. He heard footsteps but didn't bother to look behind him. By the time he got to Beach, Nash was walking alongside him, starting to ask questions. Frank stopped under a streetlight. Oscar's yellow slicker had caught most of the blood, but not all of it. Nash's leather jacket had to go. He told Nash to empty his pockets and take the jacket off.

"Jesus, Frank. It cost me three hundred and fifty bucks, and that was on sale."

"Tell Gary about it," said Frank. "Maybe he'll buy you a new one."

Nash took the jacket off, handed it to Frank. Frank dropped it on the sidewalk and kicked it under a parked car.

They went to a club on Richards Street. It seemed Frank knew the doorman. They slipped past the lineup and went straight inside, sat down at a table near the bar. There was a three-piece band. People dancing. Frank unbuttoned his jacket and then remembered the gun, buttoned the jacket back up again. He grinned at Pat Nash. "Know what a Peter Pan is?"

Nash shook his head.

"A cocktail," said Frank. "Two dashes bitters, add three-quarters of an ounce orange juice, dry vermouth and gin. Shake with ice and strain into a glass." He stood up. "Order one for me, will you?"

"Yeah, sure."

Frank pushed away from the table and disappeared into the crowd. Saturday night and the joint was jammed to the rafters, everybody hustling. Frank headed towards the washroom and then circled around to where he could watch Nash. Frank was curious. He wanted to see what Nash would do, now that he was alone. Stick tight, or beat it?

A waitress cruised by, cute little thing. Nash stuck out his leg and she glared at him, less than charmed.

Frank watched Nash's mouth move as he ordered the drinks — a Becks for himself, Frank's Peter Pan.

The waitress went away and Nash lit a cigarette and leaned his elbows on the table and eyed the ladies. Not that Frank thought he'd be in the mood for love, unless he was a lot tougher than he looked.

Frank wandered around for a few minutes, used the can, went back to the table, sat down. He took off his jacket and slung it over the back of his chair.

Nash saw the Colt was gone.

"What'd you do, flush it down the toilet?"

Frank smiled. He had a big, wide face. His smile was unexpectedly warm, full of humor. He pointed at Nash's Exports. "You mind?"

"Go ahead."

Frank shook a cigarette from the pack, ripped off the filter, struck a match.

"I thought you were gonna do me, back there," Nash said.

Frank looked over his shoulder, put a finger to his lips.

Nash turned, glanced behind him. The waitress put the Peter Pan down on the table in front of him and he pushed it away, towards Frank. She looked a little surprised, recovered quickly. Nash flushed and Frank laughed. The girl gave Nash his beer and a glass, the tab. Frank dropped a twenty-dollar bill on the table. He raised his glass. "Here's to Oscar. After all, he's paying."

Nash drained off half his Becks, taking it straight from the bottle.

Frank leaned across the table. He put his hand on Nash's arm. "Oscar had to go. He didn't have any choice, and neither did I. Understand what I'm telling you?"

"I understand."

"Guy screws up, he's gotta pay the price. Let him go, word gets out and in no time at all Gary's got people lining up to bite chunks off him." Frank let go of Nash's arm. He held his drink up to the light. "Don't get me wrong. I'm no fan. Far as I'm concerned, you want to know the truth, Gary's a first-class asshole."

Nash looked up from his beer, puzzled. It was clear he was wondering why Frank was telling him this.

Frank answered the unspoken question. "What I'm trying to tell you, don't go away mad, okay? It was a job and I had to do it. Simple as that."

Fine, said Nash's face. But why bother to explain it to me?

Figure it out, thought Frank. Use your brains, you got any. Aloud he said, "Three days, is that what Gary gave you?"

Nash nodded.

Frank drank some of his Peter Pan, wiped his mouth with a paper napkin. He balled up the napkin and tossed it on the floor. "Stay in touch, okay?"

"Okay."

"And if you get lucky, who you gonna call?"

"I'll call Gary, call him right away."

Frank helped himself to another cigarette, did the thing with the filter. Lit up. Leaned across the table with the cigarette dangling from a corner of his mouth, smoke running along the hard, bony flank of his cheek and up into his unblinking eye. He gave Nash a slip of paper with a phone number printed on it in big block letters. "Don't call Gary," he said. "Call me."

Nash drank the rest of his Becks. He was parched, the beer didn't seem to be doing a thing for him. He glanced around, wondering what the hell had happened to the waitress. And also wondering if he was getting the right message, if he and Frank were speaking the same language.

The band had taken a break but now they were back at work, music blasting out of the club's speakers, the bass so heavy it was making the floor vibrate.

Frank signalled another round of drinks. He started talking, his eyes holding Nash's, keeping his voice so low he knew it would be impossible for Nash to hear a word he was saying. Nash nodded along, doing his best to seem agreeable. His head bobbing up and down reminded Frank of one of those stuffed dogs you see in the back windows of cars driven by old people with sticky-out ears.

After about ten minutes of this, Nash excused himself and went to the can.

Frank knocked back the dregs of his Peter Pan, threw some more of Oscar's money on the table. It had been a long night. He stood up, pushed away from the table and through the crowd towards the door.

"Something wrong with the beer?"

Frank glanced up, startled. Gary was standing over him, looking pissed.

"Must've dozed off," said Frank. "It's the fire, I guess."

"Me'n Samantha are gonna go wrinkle the sheets," said Gary. "We don't make it back by the time the Jays get up to bat, tape it for me."

Frank nodded.

Gary dragged his new girlfriend out of the den. She was laughing and giggling, having a good time. But Frank knew from past experience it was a phase that wouldn't last. Gary left the door open behind him. His bedroom was down at the end of the hall. He'd leave that door open too, would expect Frank to listen carefully to all the noises he made.

Afterwards Gary'd give Frank a little quiz, twenty questions. Then he'd supply the answers. As if Frank was interested. Gary was a pervert. At times Frank was so ashamed of working for him that he didn't think he could do it any longer. But if he quit, Gary would have him killed.

So there was only one way out, really. Sooner or later, Gary had to get splashed. If Nash beat the odds and came up with the missing heroin, Frank would let him bump Gary. Nash had the best of all possible motives, revenge. So Nash'd whiff Gary, be happy to do it. And then Frank would waste Nash. Kick the Orange Julius girl's cute little ass out on the sidewalk, along with Gary's collection of cactus plants.

A happy ending, for a change.

10

Parker's apartment was on West Eleventh, just off Burrard. Willows pulled up against the curb in front of the building. He saw movement in the lobby. The door swung open. Parker, dressed in jeans, ankle-length black leather boots and a black silk jacket, came out of the building and hurried down the sidewalk towards him.

Willows smiled at her as she got into the car.

"What?" said Parker.

"You're dressed like a burglar."

"Burglars wear running shoes. Sneakers, because that's what they do. Sneak."

Willows put the Olds in gear, checked his side mirror and pulled away from the curb.

"How was court?" he said.

"Lousy. Junior got himself a very good lawyer, guy so expensive he wears a four-piece suit."

Junior was a Californian who'd strayed across the border, become involved in a shootout with Parker. He'd been wounded and spent several months in the hospital. Now he was in Oakalla, awaiting trial, and he'd applied for bail.

"He's going to make it," said Parker. "They're going to let the murderous bastard walk."

Willows shook his head, no. "He won't make bail, and they won't let him plead, either. He shot at a cop, for Chrissake."

"The lawyer claimed mitigating circumstances. We were in an unmarked car. It was dark, the light was bad. And on, and on. It was also the little scumbug's first offense. Until now, his slate was clean. Plus he's on title for that house in West Van. Which makes him a property owner. A solid citizen."

"We flashed our badges," said Willows. "He pulled his cannon and started shooting. He won't make bail. By the time he gets out, he'll be a senior citizen."

"I hope you're right," Parker said. "But I've got a hunch you're wrong."

"A hunch . . . what's that, bad posture?"

"Five dollars says Junior's home by Hallowe'en."

"I need the money," said Willows, "so I'm going to take it."

They were on the downslope of the Burrard bridge, the lights of the downtown core glittering in front of them. Willows cut to the inside lane and turned right on Beach, drove two blocks and made another right. The building site was deserted. They drove down to the lower parking lot. There were a few lights on in the condominium, but Miss Tyler's apartment was dark.

Willows stopped about twenty feet from the abandoned Cutlass. He switched on his brights and a huge, distorted shadow of the Cutlass seemed to leap from the car, cling to the concrete bridge support.

He turned off the Olds' engine but left the lights on. Flipped open the glove compartment and retrieved his police-issue flashlight, got out of the car.

There was no movement inside the Cutlass. He tried the door. It was locked. He pointed his flashlight at the car window but the encrustation of bird droppings was so thick it was impossible to see inside. He tapped on the glass with the heel of the flashlight.

"Police. Open up!"

The air was cold and damp, clammy.

Willows hit the glass with the flashlight again, but much harder. No response. He went around to the front of the car and put his foot on the bumper, pushed down. The Cutlass rocked on its springs. There was movement inside the car. The window was rolled down a couple of inches. A dark eye stared out at them.

Parker's badge was in the palm of her hand. She held it in the wash of light from Willows' car. The window was unrolled another inch.

"Wha you waa?"

The words were slurred, nearly indecipherable.

Parker spoke very slowly. "Three nights ago, did you hear a very loud sound?"

"Dea . . ."

"I can't hear you," said Parker. "I don't understand what you're saying."

The window came down a few more inches. The clean night air was filled with the sour stench of an unwashed body, sweat and fear, despair. Despite the many layers of rags that covered her and made her body a shapeless gray mass, Parker saw that the person she'd been talking to was a woman. A very old woman, by the look of her.

Willows, standing just behind Parker, played the beam of his flashlight across the woman's face. The cataracts leapt out at him. The woman touched her ears, smiled a toothless smile.

"Dea . . ." she said again.

Parker nodded. She opened her purse and got out one of her cards and a five-dollar bill.

She slipped the card and money through the crack in the window.

The window was rolled up.

Willows didn't say anything, but Parker knew exactly what he was thinking.

"Junior's going to make bail," she said. "And you're going to lose that bet."

They went back to the Oldsmobile. Willows switched off the lights. In the darkness, they walked diagonally across the gravel towards the water.

"What d'you think?" said Parker.

"About what?"

"Should we call an ambulance?"

"I wouldn't. She was rational. She looked healthy enough."

"She smelled awful."

"So would you, if you rooted around in garbage cans for a living, and never took a bath."

"What about her eyes?"

"Can't be that bad. She wouldn't have grabbed your money if she hadn't been able to see it." Willows swept the beam of his flashlight across the sailboats moored in front of the restaurant.

"We can get the beat cops to keep an eye on her, it'll make you feel better."

They passed through the gap in the chain-link fence, walked along a narrow concrete sidewalk. Willows shone his flashlight through the restaurant window. A black cat squatted on the counter by the cash register, eyes glowing bright green.

There was a gate at the top of the gangway, but it wasn't locked. Parker felt the design of the metal grid beneath the thin soles of her boots. The floating wharf shifted silently in the darkness. On either side of the narrow wooden walkway, moving water gleamed blackly.

Willows led Parker through the darkness towards one of the sailboats. The boat was about thirty feet long, painted white. Parker listened to the tinkle of aluminum rigging; a bright counterpoint to the constant hum of traffic on the bridge.

They made their way down to the stern of the boat. Willows climbed aboard first, held out a hand to Parker. The boat was dark, but when Parker held her hand over a vent, she felt hot gases, escaping heat. Willows found the hatch. It wasn't locked. He opened the hatch and crouched and peered inside.

A man and woman were lying naked on a narrow bunk, in the flickering yellow light of half a dozen candles. Willows hadn't seen any light because the portholes were covered with thick black construction paper.

The man was in his fifties, paunchy and gray. His companion was much younger; a blonde in her early twenties.

The man gaped at them. "Get the hell out of here," he yelled.

Willows stepped down into the little cuddy cabin. There was a small stainless steel stove on gimbals in the galley, both elements burning. Parker came in behind him. The stove hissed malevolently.

The man dragged a sleeping bag over his body, covered the woman even though she didn't seem concerned about her nakedness.

"Is this your boat?" said Willows.

"Get the hell out of here!" the man shouted again. His feet were sticking out of the bottom of the unzipped sleeping bag. He rubbed them together. His toenails needed clipping. He didn't sound very sure of himself.

Willows got out his badge.

There was a long silence broken only by the hiss of the stove.

"She belongs to a friend of mine," the man said at last.

"What's his name?"

"Rowland. Oliver Rowland."

"His friends call him Rollie," said the girl. She sat up. The sleeping bag fell away.

"What's your name?" Willows said to the man.

"Wayne Clark. I use the boat all the time. It's a business arrangement. I got a key, you want to see it?"

"What's your name?" Willows said to the woman.

"Wendy Lewis."

"How old are you, Miss Lewis?"

"Twenty-three."

Wayne Clark tried to look surprised. Willows didn't believe it.

"Can I see some identification, please."

Wendy Lewis' clothes were in an untidy heap at the foot of the bed. She found her purse, offered Willows her driver's licence.

Willows handed the licence back. He turned to Clark, snapped his fingers.

Wayne Clark was fifty-three years old. His marital status wasn't noted on his licence, but there was a gold band on the third finger of his left hand.

"Were you here on the boat Friday night?" Willows said.

"No."

"You're sure?"

"Absolutely."

"He's lying," said Wendy Lewis.

Clark glared at her.

A candle wavered as Willows sat down on the end of the bed.

"Spend the night?"

The girl shook her head. She ran her fingers through her hair. Were her breasts implants, or real? Willows made an effort to concentrate on the issue at hand.

"What time did you arrive?"

"A little past eight."

"In a car?"
She nodded.
"Whose car was it?"
"Mine," said Wayne Clark.
"What d'you drive, Wayne?"
"A Caddy."
"Where'd you park it?"
Clark gestured with his arm. His knuckles banged against the bulkhead. Apparently he was accustomed to making expansive gestures. "There's a paved lot behind the restaurant. It's private, but I've got a key." He sucked on his bruised fist.
"Poor baby," said Wendy Lewis. She smiled at Willows.
Willows studied the black construction paper. "Were the windows covered over on Friday?"
"Yeah."
"You said you got here at eight. Exactly when did you leave?"
"About ten."
"More like one o'clock in the morning," the girl said. "We heard the car drive up, the crash, and then the shots."
"How many shots?" said Willows.
"Two," said the girl. "Or maybe it was three."
"See anything?"
"No," said Wayne Clark.
"You heard a car crash and gunshots, but didn't get up and take a look?"
"He stuck his head under the sleeping bag," said the girl. "Like one of those big birds that can't fly. A flamingo, no, an ostrich."
"What about you, what did you do?" Parker said to Wendy Lewis.
"Went outside, took a look around."
"Stark naked," said Clark. "She wasn't even wearing a hat."
"The engine was racing, really loud. That's how I figured out where the car was, by the noise."
Willows took out his notebook, a pen.
"There were two men standing on the far side of the car. One of them knelt down and then he started walking backwards, away from the car."
"What did he look like?"

"It was dark, he was too far away, I couldn't see . . ."

"Was he tall, short . . ."

"He was big, they were both big."

"Heavy-set, thin . . ."

"Average, I guess. They weren't skinny."

"What were they wearing?"

"I don't know, I can't remember . . . Like I said, it was dark."

"The one who walked backwards away from the car, which way did he go?"

"Towards the far side of the parking lot, that new apartment block."

"What about the other man?" said Parker.

"He stayed where he was, beside the car."

"He's the one you should've had the best look at," Parker said. "Can you remember the length or color of his hair, anything at all?"

Wendy Lewis shook her head. "No, not really."

"But you could see that they were both men," said Willows.

"I *think* they were men." The girl shrugged. "But I wouldn't want to swear to it in court, if that's what you're getting at."

"Is there any chance either of them saw you?" said Willows.

"No way."

"You're sure?"

"I'd bet my life on it," said the girl. She giggled nervously.

"I'll need your home and business addresses and phone numbers, Mr Clark."

"Wait a minute now, if this . . ."

Willows gave him a look. "We phone you at home and your wife answers, we're supposed to hang up, right?"

Wayne Clark repaired typewriters for a living. He worked downtown and lived in an apartment in Kerrisdale. Willows made a mental note to get the licence number of the Caddy, just in case he was lying.

Wendy Lewis was unemployed. Willows got her home address and telephone.

"Do me a favor," she said as he put away his pen and notebook. "Pass me my panties."

"Not a chance," said Willows.

Parker was still smiling as she stood on the deck of the sailboat and watched Willows walk back to the parking lot. He stood where the car had crashed and looked for her in the darkness. Parker was wearing black, but in the incidental light from the security lamp at the top of the gangway, he was able to see the pale oval of her face, her hands.

The advantage he had over the killers was that he knew she was there and was looking for her. On the other hand, Wendy Lewis was a blonde, and her skin was very pale, and she had been naked. He started back towards the boat, to advise Clark and Lewis that they'd better find another love nest.

In the Olds, driving out from beneath the looming bulk of the bridge, Parker asked Willows if he had time for a drink.

"Sure," said Willows, diffidently.

"Forget it, some other time."

"Freddy's?" said Willows.

"That'd make a nice change."

When Willows and Freddy had first met, Freddy'd been cuffed to a skid-row radiator, his left hand spouting blood. The hand had been stuffed in a blender, the three middle fingers chewed off right down to the knuckle. Years later, he'd told Willows of the horror he'd felt as he'd watched the glass wall of the blender turn bright red and then pink, chunks of raw flesh swirling and spinning. Now, years later, the stumps were white as a glacier, covered in a mass of scar tissue slick as ice.

The lost fingers had a remarkable effect on Freddy, calmed him down. Six months after it happened, he flew the redeye to Reno and married his business partner and barmaid, Sally.

In the chapel there was a moment of panic, and then Sally slipped the wedding ring over Freddy's thumb.

Freddy had been married almost two years now, but still hadn't lost his eye for women. Parker was at the top of his wish-list. He spotted her as she walked in the door, and reached for the bottle of Cutty Sark. She wasn't the kind of woman who liked to drink alone. He was sure Willows would be right behind her.

Freddy was right.

Willows nodded at Freddy as he walked past the bar, held up two fingers and rotated his hand to indicate a pouring motion.

Doubles.

Freddy poured the drinks freehand, carried them down the length of the bar to the end booth. Dropped napkins on the table and put down the drinks.

"Thanks, Freddy."

"We got a special on chicken wings. Interested?"

"I'll pass."

Freddy shook his head, stared gloomily down at the floor. "Brother, what a week."

Willows sipped his drink.

Freddy turned to Parker. "Brother," he said, "what a week."

"Problem?" said Parker.

Willows glanced up at her across the rim of his glass, gave her a look.

"Sally's always liked to read in bed. Usually it's only a magazine, or maybe the newspaper. But since last Sunday, she's been dragging the *Encyclopaedia Britannica* into the sack with her. And I'm not talking about one volume, either. I mean the whole goddamn . . ."

"Stop," said Willows.

"You heard it?"

Willows nodded.

"Pretty good, eh?"

"A real side-splitter, Freddy."

"Laughed until I cried, swear to God."

"*I* haven't heard it," said Parker.

"Ask *him* to tell it to you," said Freddy, indicating Willows with a disdainful jerk of his thumb.

Parker said, "The boys in fraud tell me you water your drinks."

"With my tears," said Freddy. He gave the table a brisk wipe and walked away.

"You get the forensics on the Pontiac?" said Willows.

"Jerry Goldstein called in sick. We got shoved to the bottom of the pile."

Willows opened his mouth but, whatever he was about to say, thought better of it.

"Hey," said Parker, "don't blame me."

Willows drank some Cutty.

"It'll be on your desk first thing in the morning. They promised."

"I'll bet they did."

"I phoned Jerry at home, told him to call his staff and get them off their asses."

"That must have cheered him up."

Parker tasted her Scotch, put the glass back down on the table. "Orwell talked to the kid who worked on the Aquabus. Kid's name is Steve Bromley. He didn't see or hear a thing, didn't even know there'd been a murder until Orwell told him about it."

"Why'd he quit work?"

"Had an argument with his boss."

"Eddy believed him?"

"Every last word." Parker swirled the ice in her drink. "Tell me something, Jack."

Willows waited.

Parker took a mouthful of Scotch, gulped it down. "How're you getting along with your wife?"

Willows leaned back in his seat. "Okay, I guess."

"*Okay*?" said Parker.

"Not too bad."

"She still in Toronto?"

"Yeah."

Parker reached across the table. Lightly traced her fingers across the back of Willows' hand.

Willows drained his glass. Not looking at her, he said, "You want another drink?"

"But not here, okay."

Willows reached for his jacket.

"My place," said Parker. "It's closer."

"Tidier too, I bet."

"For the time being," Parker said.

11

The door rattled against the frame. Paterson went for the Ruger, held the gun down low against his hip. He sat up. The bedsprings creaked. He felt ridiculous — a character in a melodrama, an old black and white movie. He stuck the Ruger back in the pocket of his jacket and said, "Who is it?"

"Room service, pal."

The nightclerk, rumpled and ironic. Paterson imagined him leaning against the wall, thumb hooked in the waistband of his jeans. He said, "Come on in."

The door swung open and a man slipped into the room like a shadow, silent and fluid. His skin was the color of smoked glass, smooth and gleaming. He was about six feet tall, and very thin. He had on a dark blue poplin trenchcoat, black leather gloves, tight black pants and shiny black patent leather shoes. The shoes were small, about a size eight. The collar of the trenchcoat was turned up, the belt cinched tight. He was shaved bald; there was a razor cut above his left ear, another nick at the base of the skull. The guy looked theatrical and dumb — but very scary.

Paterson stood up. He tried not to think about how stupid he'd been, wished that the Ruger was still in his hand. A woman stepped into the room. He began to relax. The woman stayed just inside the door, her back to the wall. She was white, wearing a sequined jean jacket, tight yellow skirt, mesh nylons. Her hair was a bright, garish orange, shot through with streaks of green. She glanced at Paterson and then looked away, disinterested.

The man danced lightly across the room, stopped near the foot of the bed.

"Shut the door, Moira."

The woman shut the door.

Paterson stood there by the bed, waiting, not quite sure how to handle the situation. He decided to let the pimp make the first move, follow his lead.

As if reading his mind, the man pointed a gloved finger at him and said, "Relax, baby. I'm Moira's talent agent, her manager. The name's Randall."

Randall stared at the bulge in Paterson's pocket. "Carrying some weight, baby?"

"I told the nightclerk I wanted three women."

"Pete don't count too good. You a cop?"

Paterson shook his head.

"Humor me, baby. Say it out loud. Then I don't gotta worry about entrapment, any of that shit."

"I'm not a cop."

"Well, that makes two of us." Randall stuck a finger in his ear, poked and prodded, studied what he'd caught beneath the nail. "Three girls at once, huh." He moved a little closer. "Tell me something, does it matter how old they are?"

"Not particularly."

"Color?"

Paterson shrugged.

"Reason I ask, tell you the truth, is you look as if you could barely handle one of my sweet ladies, much less a trio."

"I want to meet a junkie."

"A *what*? A junkie? Why is that?"

"I'm writing a magazine article."

"You're a fucking writer?"

"Yeah."

Randall stared down at him. Eyes cold and shiny as his patent leather shoes. "I don't get it, man. What is it, somebody worked the numbers and told you one out of three hookers bound to be wired?"

"Simple as that," said Paterson. He wondered if he looked as terrified as he felt. He wanted to sit down, but the way Randall was standing there, it didn't seem like a very good idea.

"Bullshit, baby. That ain't no pen you got in your pocket, it's a fuckin' bazooka."

Paterson hesitated. He pulled out the Ruger, held the pistol with the barrel in his left hand.

Moira made a small sound of dismay. "Shut the fuck up," said Randall, not bothering to look at her. To Paterson he said, "What is that thing, a twenty-two?"

"Yeah."

"Got a silencer on it?"

"Bull barrel," said Paterson. "For target shooting. The extra weight minimizes the recoil."

Randall scratched the razor cut on the back of his neck. He began to bleed. He sucked blood from his finger. "You gonna splash me, that it?"

"What?"

"Forget it." Randall giggled. He flapped his hands in a gesture of dismissal. "What you really want, man. Or do you even fuckin' know?"

"I want to sell some heroin," said Paterson.

Randall hesitated. "Sell, or buy?"

"Sell."

"How much we talkin' about?"

"Twenty kilos," said Paterson. "A little more than forty-four pounds."

"I know how much a fucking key weighs, goddammit!" Randall studied the gun in Paterson's lap. "You shittin' me, man?"

"No, of course not."

Randall nodded. He'd heard Gary Silk had suffered a major loss, but he hadn't had any idea how big it was. "It here with you?"

"Sorry, Randall."

Randall grinned, showing small teeth and lots of gum. "Where you got it stashed, man?"

"That's a million-dollar question, Randall. You got the cash you need to buy the answer?"

"Tell me something, babe. You started out on this here day trip, you remember to load your gun?"

"With hollowpoints. Want one, Randy?"

Randall held up his hands, palms out. "Maybe later. Wouldn't mind a little taste of the merchandise, though."

"In the bathroom, down at the end of the hall. On the floor behind the toilet."

"Got it all worked out, huh?"

"This's way too big for you, Randy. Go-between's the best you can do. Somebody you know might be interested, I'll be at the Sunrise Hotel until they close the bar."

"The Sunrise."

"One night only. Then I'm gone."

"Go get Walt," said Randall. Moira frowned. "He's in the fuckin' car," Randall said. "C'mon baby, get yo' pretty little ass in gear." Moira yanked open the door. Her heels clattered on the linoleum.

"Wait a minute," said Paterson.

Randall went over to the door and kicked it shut, leaned against the frame with his arms folded across his chest. He said, "Easy, now. Don't do nothin' foolish."

Paterson pointed the Ruger at Randall's face. "Get the hell away from that door."

"Or you'll blow my head off, right?" Randall reached inside his trenchcoat, took out a pack of Virginia Slims. He offered the pack to Paterson. "Smoke?"

Paterson forced himself to move towards the window. His legs felt stiff, as if they were made of wood.

"What'd I say?" said Randall.

Paterson tried to yank open the window, but it was stuck, nailed shut. He used the butt of the gun to smash the glass.

"Don't get me mad, baby. I lose my temper, something real bad could happen."

Paterson kept working at the glass.

Randall pulled a butterfly knife, flicked it open. "Back off, baby."

Paterson used his elbow to clear away the last shards of glass. He crouched, managed to get his left leg and part of his lower body out the window. Randall lit his cigarette and then came at him, moving incredibly fast.

The Ruger exploded. Randall skidded to a stop. The cigarette fell out of his mouth. He lifted the hem of his tight-belted trenchcoat and touched the bloody hole in his pants, high up on the meaty part of his thigh.

"You shot me, you dink. And you ruined my fuckin' pants."

"Jesus," said Paterson, "it was an accident."

Randall leapt at him.

Paterson yanked the trigger three times and then managed to regain control. Randall was rolling around on the floor clutching his knee, screaming.

There were shouts in the hallway.

Paterson jammed the Ruger into his pocket, climbed the rest of the way through the shattered window. Blood bubbled from a long cut on the side of his thumb. He started down the fire escape towards the black hole of the alley.

Behind him, Randall had stopped screaming and started shouting. Wood splintered. The light was blocked as someone leaned out the window. Paterson's foot slipped on one of the metal rungs. He snatched at the railing with his left hand, felt a sharp, dizzying spasm of pain.

Rusty metal trembled. He looked up. There were two of the bastards, and they were coming after him.

The fire escape stopped about ten feet above ground level. The ladder had a fold-down section but it was stuck. Directly below him there was a dumpster. He let himself drop, hit sheet steel, fell to his knees, jumped to the asphalt. The dumpster was small, and had wheels. He gave it a push and it rolled down the alley, away from the fire escape.

The alley was in the shape of a T. Hastings Street was less than a hundred feet away. He turned to run. The lights of a car parked in the mouth of the alley switched on, blinding him. He went left, into darkness. There was the roar of an engine, a shouted oath, the screech of brakes. The alley was flooded with light. A man came around the corner. He shouted incomprehensible words and extended his right arm.

Fifty feet down the alley a solitary house was squeezed in between a row of featureless flat-roofed brick buildings. Paterson ducked into the back yard, ran past a rusty Datsun pickup truck, up a flight of wooden stairs to the back porch. The door was locked. He heard footsteps slam down the alley. A narrow stairway led upwards. He began to climb. There was a tiny door under the peak of the roof, something from *Alice In Wonderland*. He tried the knob, kicked hard. The door was solid, unyielding.

The beam of a flashlight lanced upwards. He got a foot on the doorknob, reached up and levered himself on to the steeply-sloped roof. A loose shingle fluttered into the darkness.

"Get the bastard!" Randall's voice. Paterson felt a shudder of relief; he thought he'd killed him.

Crouching low, he crept along the roof to the front of the house, then let himself slide down until he could jump across the foot-wide gap between the house and the adjoining building. The beam of the flashlight wavered in the air, as if celebrating an uncertain event. He trotted across the flat, tar-and-gravel roof to the far side of the building. There was a false front, a narrow ledge about two feet high. He peered over the ledge. The car was a black Lincoln. The lights were off but the engine was running.

Paterson moved away from the car, towards the far end of the building. About halfway down the length of the building a telephone pole stood within a few inches of the wall. A tangle of loose electrical wire made climbing impossible, but there was a black plastic drainpipe next to the pole and when he yanked on it he found that it was firm, fixed in place with metal bands and steel bolts.

He hesitated, then swung his legs over the parapet and started to shinny down the pipe. His pants snagged on something. He glanced down and saw that the lower part of the pipe had been wrapped in barbed wire. He yanked his leg free, got set.

Jumped.

The shock of impact ran all the way up his body. His head snapped forward, chin on knee. He tasted blood.

The Lincoln's brake lights flashed red. He broke into a run, his shadow spilling behind him across the cobbled lane, overtaking him as he passed beneath a streetlight.

He reached a cross street, Cordova. The warehouses and office buildings on either side were dark, deserted. To his left there was an apartment. He sprinted across the brightly-lit street. The door to the complex was locked. There was a list of tenants, an intercom. He slapped at the small black buttons.

No response.

He turned and ran up Cordova. The Lincoln slid out of the mouth of the alley on the far side of the street. He ran down the alley, heard a squeal of rubber, turned sharply left and ran past the rear of the building.

His foot hit an empty pressurized Lysol can and sent it clattering down the alley. A part of his mind remembered reading somewhere that skid-road alcoholics mixed the liquid with Coke and then drank it and often died.

Behind the apartment block there was an open, grassy area. A tall, white-painted metal fence had been built to keep out the Lysol drinkers. He climbed the fence and dropped. Lights shaped like giant question marks made pools of light on the grass. Lungs aching, he ran towards a second, smaller block of apartments, and an exterior stairway surrounded by metal scaffolding that led all the way to the top floor. Behind him there was a shout of triumph. He glanced over his shoulder and saw the Lincoln speeding towards him in reverse. Two men were climbing the gate. A third was crouched on the far side of the alley.

He heard a sound like someone spitting. A bullet hit one of the lights, whined into the night with the sound of a mechanized mosquito. He stood motionless, in shock. A bullet smacked into the brick wall of the building. He thought they'd been shooting at his legs, but now he wasn't so sure.

One of the men on the fence dropped to the ground and trotted towards him in a shallow arc that kept him out of the line of fire.

Paterson scurried up the stairs, climbing as fast as he could. His hand throbbed. His chest was on fire. He stumbled, fell, picked himself up.

He reached a landing and tried the door. Locked. A man walked down the hallway towards him. He pounded on the door, leaving splashes of blood on the glass. The man stopped in front of an apartment door, produced a key. The door swung open and in the brighter light that came from within, Paterson saw that he was carrying a portable tape player equipped with earphones.

The man disappeared into the apartment, shut the door behind him.

Paterson could hear his pursuers climbing towards him, closing the gap. He hurried up the stairs to the next landing. Two more storeys and there'd be nowhere else to go, he'd be trapped. He reached for the door, saw as his fingers touched the metal handle that it was slightly ajar. He yanked the door open and slammed it shut behind him, heard the click of the automatic lock.

He hurried down the hallway. His hand was bleeding badly, leaving a spoor of blood on the floor behind him. He found the stairway. Above and behind him he heard glass shattering, shouts. He hurried down the stairs, taking them two and three at a time, lost his balance and automatically threw out his arm, painted a wide smear of blood on the white-painted wall.

A few moments later he reached ground level. The front entrance was about twenty feet down the hall. He hurried to the door and looked out. The Lincoln could be anywhere. He pushed the door open and went outside. Moonlight shone on the complex of railway tracks on the other side of Alexandria, and in the distance he could hear the snort and whistle of a diesel engine.

Clutching his injured hand, he ran down the concrete steps to the street and hurried across Alexandria, past a small white building, a tiny restaurant. To the left of the restaurant there was a Hydro junction box with a big red sticker on it that said DANGER HIGH VOLTAGE. He got up on the box and clambered awkwardly over the chain-link fence that separated the road from the railway tracks, jogged across gleaming streaks of metal towards a squat two-storey building.

There was a shout from the street. The Lincoln swung in a half circle, headlights carving an arc through the night. He crouched, ran headlong into another fence. He stumbled, fell to his knees. A sign on the side of the building read PORTS CANADA POLICE. He veered away from the building and across a paved access road, up a grassy slope.

He was at Crab Park, the only waterfront park that serviced the city's East Side. A block away, the Lincoln sped over the steeply-sloped bridge that ran from the foot of Main Street over the train tracks and parallel to the harbor. Paterson trotted across the grass towards the glistening black expanse of water.

He heard voices, but couldn't tell what direction they were coming from. It occurred to him that he had been running in a straight line since he'd crossed the road. He swerved left. In front of him there was an area of low ground, thicker darkness.

He ran a few more yards. Stones beneath his feet made a sound like teeth grinding together. He had stumbled upon a small pond, was surrounded by tall, gently rustling bulrushes. Behind him, silhouetted against the lights of the Ports Canada building, were the blurred shapes of three running men.

He crouched down. The beam of a flashlight swept low, was quickly extinguished. His heart lurched. With the light, they could easily follow his trail across the dew-laden grass.

He glanced warily around. The run had left him feeling as if a knitting needle had been driven between his ribs. He blinked, wiped his eyes with the back of his hand. The harbor was off to his left. He could double back the way he'd come but if they saw him he'd be trapped. He decided to go west, follow the waterfront.

He took a deep breath, stood up and began to run.

On the far side of the pond there was a parking lot the size of a city block. He hurdled endless rows of white lines, heels thumping on the asphalt. He jumped a ditch, struggled across a field of mud. A hundred yards in front of him there was a chain-link fence and lights that shone down from tall orange and white striped poles. Mud sucked at his shoes, tried to drag him down.

Shoes squelching in the soft mud, he turned towards the railway tracks.

A diesel engine thundered slowly down the track. He started running again. Off to his right, green and red lights rippled on the water. The lights were from the commuter ferry that crossed the harbor from the old CPR terminal at the foot of Granville to North Vancouver's Londsdale Quay. He realized he was only a few hundred feet from the terminal.

Behind him there was a flash of orange light, that spitting sound again.

He saw the fence a fraction of a second before he ran into it, hooked his fingers into the mesh and began to climb. His shoes were slippery with mud. He managed to hook a leg over the top. Something clutched at his ankle. He kicked blindly out. There was a cry of pain, thud of a body hitting the ground. He let himself drop, rolled to his feet and ran for his life, wheezed across another stretch of muddy ground.

There were two sets of double glass doors in the corrugated metal wall of the Seabus terminal. A sticker on each door declared EMERGENCY EXIT ONLY. NO ACCESS.

Paterson stepped back and kicked the glass panel with all the strength he had left in him. The glass exploded in a greenish-white froth. He stepped through the door. A number of people riding the UP escalator that serviced the enclosed walkway spanning the railway tracks stared at him in mute disbelief. Passengers, he realized, from the boat he'd seen in the harbor. He ran towards the dock. Turnaround time was very fast; the ferries stayed in berth for only a few minutes. If he didn't make the connection, there was nowhere else to go.

He ran down a long, gently descending ramp towards the smell of the ocean, diesel fumes. The ferry's access doors were still open. He was only a few steps away when they began to close. He yelled his dismay. A fat kid wearing frayed jeans, a white T-shirt and a black leather jacket stuck out his booted foot. The shiny plate-glass doors banged against the boot and then rebounded, sliding open again. Paterson threw himself across a short metal ramp. The kid had a James Dean haircut. He gave Paterson a cheerful grin. The doors slid shut.

Paterson sat down in a seat made of molded gray fiberglass.

"Holy shit," said the kid.

Paterson lifted his head. There were two men on the ramp. One of them was trying to pry the doors apart. His face was twisted with the effort, and his palms and the pads of his fingers were white on the glass. His companion had a gun, a black pistol. He pointed it at Paterson and gestured with his free hand, telling him to stand up, come towards him.

The engines throbbed. Hydraulics slowly began to raise the ramp to a vertical position. The men were forced to jump down to the dock. The one with the gun fell to his knees, clutched at his companion. He stood up, trotted alongside the ferry as it moved out of the slip towards open water.

Paterson was frozen, immobile. He sat motionless as the man with the gun followed him all the way down to the end of the dock. The ferry moved into open water, began to pick up speed. The gunman aimed at Paterson and then smiled and waved goodbye.

There were only about a dozen passengers on board the Seabus. No one seemed to have noticed anything.

"How long till we get to the other side?" Paterson said.

"They had a fucking gun!" said the kid, and giggled shrilly.

Paterson grabbed a leather-clad arm, squeezed hard. "How long is it going to take us to get across, Jimmy?"

"I dunno. Ten, maybe fifteen minutes."

Paterson nodded. He'd lost them. For the time being at least, he was safe.

12

Jerry Goldstein was in his late thirties but still had a full head of curly blond hair, the complexion of a choir boy, a smile that resembled nothing quite so much as a cheerful jumbled landslide of sharp white teeth. Virtually everyone who met him was reminded of a young Paul Newman. His resemblance to the famous American actor was largely due to his intensely vivid blue eyes, which were artificially — and secretly — enhanced by tinted contact lenses. Unlike Newman, however, Goldstein wasn't color-blind.

Today, for the first time in his working life, he wasn't wearing his contacts. The effect was little short of catastrophic. The lively, sparkling blue of a summer sky had faded overnight to the washed-out color of a pair of raggedy old jeans. It was as if Goldstein had changed his name to Dorian Gray. Overnight, his eyes had lost their lustre, their lust for life.

Willows, leaning against the desk in Goldstein's dusty, lidless glass box of an office down at the far end of the crime lab, got straight to the point. "Lose your contacts, Jerry?"

The worn crochet cushion shifted beneath Goldstein's buttocks; his captain's chair squeaked in dismay. He critically scrutinized his cuticles, drummed his knuckles on the steel surface of his desk. Finally he said, "I decided not to wear them anymore."

"Why not?" said Parker.

"Too dangerous."

"Yeah," said Willows. "I remember reading about a guy who was attacked by a contact lens."

"You know how many times a day the average person blinks?" said Goldstein. "Thousands. And every time you blink, your contact lenses shift across the surface of your eyes. Know how far the average lens travels during the course of a single day?"

Willows and Parker exchanged a look. Willows could tell by

the way Parker's eyes were squinched up that she was trying not to laugh. "A long way, I bet," Willows said.

"The length of a football field," replied Goldstein promptly. "More than a hundred yards. Constantly moving back and forth, back and forth. Think about it. What do we get when two surfaces rub against each other?"

By way of example, he pressed his palms together and made a brisk scrubbing motion, his watchband gleaming in the overhead fluorescents.

"Heat?" said Parker.

Goldstein smiled. Parker blushed.

"Friction, Claire. And when you've got something as hard as plastic pressing up against something as soft as the tissue of a human eye . . . You wear contacts, don't you?"

"No," said Parker.

"Your eyes are naturally that dark?"

Parker nodded. Goldstein stared at her as if he couldn't quite make up his mind whether to believe her or not. He'd replaced his contacts with a pair of heavy, black-plastic framed glasses with lenses thick as a TV screen, that looked about twenty years old. He took the glasses off and polished them with a Kleenex. There were red marks on the bridge of his nose, little pressure indentations on his cheekbones in front of his ears. Behind him, the brain of a famous mass-murderer floated benignly in a jar of cloudy liquid. Parker remembered reading somewhere that the brains of all creatures, including humans, had the same caloric rating — about 150 calories per ounce. Why would she bother to remember such a useless piece of information, instead of, say, her postal code? "The shooting down at the foot of Granville Street," she said. "What have you got for us?"

Goldstein replaced his glasses, got them aligned to his satisfaction on the bridge of his nose. He leaned forward in his chair, consulted a pad of lined yellow paper.

"I assume the situation is static, that we're still looking for a corpse?"

"High and low," said Willows.

"There was only one blood type in the Pontiac," said Goldstein. "O positive. The brain tissue was human, and the bone fragments probably came from a human skull." He paused. "I can't be certain about that last point. A guy named Waters, physical anthropologist out at UBC, has agreed to take a look. He's one of the best in his field. Said he'd know if the bones were human by the day after tomorrow. If it is, you're looking at murder. No one could survive that kind of wound."

"We'd assumed from the start that it was something a little more serious than a nosebleed," said Willows.

Goldstein nodded. "There was quite a bit of hair in the car, some of it attached to flesh. The victim was caucasian, definitely a male."

"Can you give us an approximate age?" said Parker.

"Not with what we've got. If I had more bones, the rest of the skull or part of the spinal cord, I might be able to do something."

"Prints?"

"Nothing. That car was wiped cleaner than a . . ." He trailed off, glanced at Parker, looked quickly away.

"What else?" said Willows.

"From my point of view, Jack, the first thing you should do is find the body. The body would definitely be an asset. Judging from the crime scene, I'd say the shooting was done at point-blank range. It turns out the body's in good shape, I'd expect to find evidence of smoke particles, lubricants, grime from the barrel."

Goldstein turned a page in his notebook, squinted, adjusted his glasses. "Now you're gonna ask me about the spent twenty-five and forty-five calibre shells you found, aren't you?"

"What about them?" said Willows.

"Like we figured, the guns were automatics, a Star and a Colt. But other than that, nothing."

"No prints on the shell casings?"

"They were clean."

"Not even a partial? Were they wiped clean?"

"I'd say so, yeah."

Goldstein removed his glasses, peered worriedly at the lenses.

"Problem?" said Parker.

"Last time I wore these was in pre-med. They're scratched all to hell, and I can't pick up my new ones until tomorrow afternoon." He put the glasses back on. "You found a witness, I heard."

Willows cocked an eyebrow.

"The bag lady," said Goldstein. "The woman living in the Cutlass."

"She was deaf, Jerry, and half-blind. She saw no evil."

"Not that she'd admit to."

"You know something I don't?"

"From what I heard, you could've pushed her a little harder, that's all. Maybe dragged her down to detox, let her spend a couple of nights in the tank." Goldstein smiled. "Put a hook on her mobile home. Squeeze her a little, see what comes out."

"I've tried squeezing people like her," said Willows. "What comes out are tears, Jerry."

"Hey, it's your case."

"That's right," said Parker. She gave Goldstein a look: worm in apple.

"Just trying to help, that's all. I mean, you don't have a victim *or* a suspect. But you seem to think you can toss me a hank of hair and a piece of bone, stand back and wait for another miracle on Main Street. Well, let me tell you something, I'm a forensic scientist, not the goddamn Wizard of Oz."

"Thanks for your help," said Willows.

Goldstein slammed the door behind them. The glass panels shivered, but held.

"What was that all about?" said Parker.

"His wife's pregnant," said Willows. "She had an amnio. It looks like twins."

"Really?"

"They were going to go to Europe this summer. Trip of a lifetime. They've been saving for years."

"And now it's off?"

Willows nodded.

"The poor guy," said Parker.

Willows gave her a puzzled look.

"What? What is it?"

"I thought you'd be all over him for not anticipating the thrill of fatherhood."

"What is he, about thirty-five?"

"Thirty-nine."

"By the time the kids are old enough to travel, he'll be in his mid-forties. Probably by then they won't be able to afford the trip in the first place, but even if they do manage to go, it won't be the romantic holiday they wanted. He'll spend the whole trip listening to the twins tell him what a rotten time they're having."

"You sound as if you've given it a lot of thought."

"When my parents took my sister and I to Europe," said Parker, "I was so bored I thought I was going to die."

Willows checked his watch. "Want some lunch?"

"I'm not hungry."

"All the better. It won't cost as much to feed you."

They walked up Main to Keefer, turned right and went past one of the BC Tel booths that had been made to look like somebody's idea of a miniature Chinese pagoda. "The Green Dragon all right?" said Willows.

"It'll do."

They strolled side by side down the sloping sidewalk, past clothing and jewelry stores, several restaurants. A row of barbecued ducks hung in the window of a butcher's shop, their slick brown bodies kept at a temperature the city's health inspectors periodically insisted was certain to result in food poisoning. So far, after more than a century of good eating, no one had complained.

Willows pushed the restaurant's glass door open, held it for Parker. A waiter wearing baggy pants and a white shirt led them to a booth. Willows sat facing the door. The waiter dropped menus on the table and started to wander off. Willows called him back.

"Chicken Chop Suey, for two. Diet Cokes. A bowl of steamed rice."

"You want chopsticks?"

"Please."

"Tell me again," said Parker. "What is it about this place that you like?"

"The ambiance."

Parker glanced around. The walls were painted a dull, scabrous green. The linoleum was so badly worn she couldn't even tell what color it was. Although it was late August, last year's Christmas decorations still hung from the bile-yellow ceiling.

The waiter returned with the chopsticks and cans of Coke, a couple of red and white striped straws.

"Could I have a glass, please?" said Parker. She turned to Willows. "You want a glass, Jack?"

Willows grunted. Had there been two killers? Or had the .25 belonged to the man who'd been shot? If the gun had been fired in self-defense, maybe it was the guy with the .45 who'd been hit. Willows popped the tab on his Coke, sipped thoughtfully. Goldstein was right. He needed a body. Until he had a body, he had nothing.

13

"Tell me what happened, Randy."

"I already told Frank. Didn't he tell you?"

Gary said, "How'd you get those cuts on the back of your head?"

"Shaving."

"What kind of razor you use?"

"I dunno. Those ones you use two or three times, throw 'em away."

Gary nodded, waited for more.

"Bright orange," said Randall. "In a four-pack, wrapped in plastic. You can get 'em anywhere . . . the corner store . . ." He searched his mind for the right word, found it at last. "Disposable."

"You're bleeding. Did you know you were bleeding, Randy?"

"Sometimes I cut myself. It happens. But it don't bother me, I got a high pain threshold, half the time I don't even know it happened."

"What is it you got stuck on there, toilet paper?"

"Kleenex," said Randall. He sounded hurt, as if Gary had insulted him.

"When'd you last do that to yourself?"

"Do what?"

"Shave."

"This morning, about ten."

"And you're still leaking blood? What's the problem, can't stop picking at the scabs?"

Gary stared at Randall DesMoines for a moment, and then sighed and looked away, into the orange and red depths of the gas flames dancing in the fireplace. Was hell really like the inside of a great big furnace, all hot and scorchy? Maybe he should tell Frank to stick Randall's bald head in there, burn a little sense into him.

"Frank?"

"Yeah, Gary?"

"Forget it." Gary sipped at his Molson Lite. Beside him on the couch, Samantha was busy peeling an orange. Gary watched her split the rind and then use her thumbnail to bulldoze the white gunk that clung to the inside skin.

"Frank?"

"Yeah, Gary?"

"What's that white gunk called, that she's digging at with her fingernails?"

"Beats me," said Frank.

Gary watched her segment the orange. Take a big bite. Juice, sticky and cold, squirted out of her mouth and across Gary's arm.

"Hey, baby, I already had a shower."

Samantha leaned over, took his arm and held it up to her mouth, licked him clean. Gary liked, really and truly liked, the feel of her tongue, febrile and wet, as it glided smoothly across his skin, flattening the coarse black hair on his wrist. He smirked at Frank but Frank was studying the ceiling.

Gary turned his attention to Randall, small-time drug dealer and part-time pimp, full-time halfwit. "You're right, Randy. You told Frank and he told me. But now I want to hear it from your own sweet lips. Then, if I feel like it, I can tell Frank. And we'll all have had a turn. See my point?"

"Sure thing, Mr Silk." Randall cleared his throat, sipped at his gin and tonic.

Gary could see he was a little confused, needed a cue. "You got a call from the nightclerk at the hotel," Gary said. "Then what happened?"

"I went over there and up to a room and met this guy who said he wanted three women. For research. Told me he was a writer, doing a thing on dope addicts. I asked him what he really had in mind. Said he had some smack he wanted to sell, there was a sample stashed down the hall in the . . ."

"Wait a minute, hold it. Why the broads?"

"It's hard to figure," said Randall. "I think his idea was that most hookers are junkies, so it was a way of making a connection."

"Fucking idiot. What happened next?"

"Told me he had a stash hidden down the hall, in the john. About half an ounce. I sent my woman after it, Moira. You ever met her?"

Gary shook his head, no. And he probably didn't want to, come to think of it.

"While she was gone, the guy started getting antsy. After a couple minutes he decided to take a walk."

"And you tried to stop him. So he shot you."

"In the leg, Mr Silk. Twice." Randall touched his bandaged knee.

"You're a tough cookie, Randall." Gary shook his head in apparent admiration. Frank had told him about the wounds. Randy'd caught the first bullet, a .22, in the fatty part of the thigh. Through and through, nice and clean. The second round had grazed his knee; he'd lost some skin but that was about it. Gary wasn't too impressed. He'd never been shot himself, but he didn't imagine it hurt all that much. Frank, on the other hand, had been hit on two separate occasions, the first time in the small of the back, second time in the chest. Both rounds had been big-bore stuff — a cop's .38 wadcutter and the one in the chest a .357 Magnum fired by some clown Frank had never seen before or since, who'd taken down a poker game on the one night out of a thousand Frank had been a winner. Gary had noticed the wounds in the hot tub. Puckered white flesh, shiny and hard with scar tissue. The .38 had been the bad one, collapsed a lung. Frank hadn't wanted to talk about it but Gary had drawn him out. Gary stared at Randall DesMoines, who'd spend the rest of his life bragging about what a hard-ass he was. Slimy little creep. Probably his idea of a good restaurant was some place where you could find lots of gum stuck under the table.

"After you got shot," said Gary, "then what?"

"The guy went out the window, climbed down the fire escape. My boys went after him. I gave the room a quick toss and got the hell out of there."

"You didn't think it was a good idea to stick around, see if he might come back?"

"Like I told you, I'd been shot. Was bleeding all over the goddamn place."

"Still are," said Gary. He gave Frank a wink.

Randall took a hit from his gin and tonic and snuck a quick look at Gary's girlfriend, the cute blonde with the tight sweater and loose mouth. Her name was Samantha but Gary called her Sam. Why would Gary change her name so it made her sound like a boy? Weird. "Even a small-bore handgun makes a hell of a racket, Mr Silk. I figured somebody must've called the cops."

"Okay, you left the hotel. Then what?"

"I went back to my place."

"Where's that, Randall?"

"China Creek. I got an apartment there, a condo. Two bedroom and den, top floor. Nobody walking around on my head. Quiet."

"Cable TV, too, I bet."

Randall nodded, hesitant.

Frank chuckled softly.

"So you went home and watched an old Bogart movie, is that it?"

"No, I watched Moira do the dope."

"Shoot up the free sample from the Vance."

"Yeah, right."

"You weren't worried it might turn out to be baking powder, icing sugar or whatever. Lye, maybe?"

"Moira gave it a taste. Said it tasted good."

"Yeah, I'll bet it did." Sam had broken a wedge of orange in half and was rubbing it across Gary's arm, the back of his hand, his fingers. Her tongue flicked at him, slurp slurp. He moved away from her. His gold chains clinked softly. He said, "Gimme ten minutes, go take a shower."

"Okay," said Samantha.

Gary watched her walk out of the room and then turned back to the idiot. "So Moira shot up, yes?"

"Right," said Randall. "She was dead inside of, like maybe five minutes. I found her in the bathroom, sitting on the toilet. It's a narrow space in there, between the toilet and the tub. She's leaning against the wall, eyes wide open, staring up at the goddamn light fixture."

"Died of an overdose, you're telling me?"

"A hot shot. The junk hadn't been stepped on, was pure as Ivory Snow." Randall glanced at Gary. "She had a big smile on her face, I'm pretty sure she died happy."

"That must be a relief."

"We were together a long time, me'n Moira. I'm gonna miss her."

"The guy who popped you, what happened to him?"

"We lost him down by the waterfront."

"He had a car?"

"No, he was on foot."

"But your guys had a car, didn't they?" Gary smiled. "Big shot like you, Randall, I hope you didn't tell them to take the fucking bus."

"There was four of them, Mr Silk. Three on foot and one in my Lincoln. The guy was jumping fences, running in and out of buildings. It's warehouses and all that shit down there. Dark."

"Tell me at least that you almost had him," said Gary. "Tell me it was close."

"It was really close," said Randall. He drained his gin and tonic and stared at the empty glass. Gary didn't say anything. Frank looked solemn, distracted. Randall tilted his glass and chewed on a piece of ice.

"Tell you the truth Randall, I'm a little pissed off."

"I'm sorry, Mr Silk. I did the best I could."

"Being sorry doesn't make it better. Right, Frank?"

"Absolutely."

"On the street, that dope is worth eighty million dollars," said Gary. He went over to the bar and grabbed a can of Lite out of the fridge, poured the beer into a clean glass, sipped, watched the bubbles. "Frank, go get a flashlight."

Frank pushed away from the mantel and went out of the room. He left the door open behind him. Randall could hear his footsteps, heavy and measured, fading down the hall. He guessed Frank's height at about six foot six, his weight at maybe three hundred pounds. Randall had heard rumours that Frank had done at least five people for Gary, including a twelve-year-old kid who'd happened to be in the wrong place at the wrong time. He'd seen a *Crimestoppers* thing about the kid on TV, re-enactment of the crime. Kid had been doing his paper route. It was something like six o'clock in the morning, just after Christmas and still pretty dark at that time of year. The way Randall heard it, the guy Frank had done was a musician, played tenor sax. Out all night and Frank had waited up for him, shot him dead while he was singing in the shower.

Then Frank had come out of the apartment and the kid was standing there with a canvas bag of newspapers under his arm. Frank had strangled him with the bag's shoulder strap. The reward had hit thirty grand, but Frank worked for Gary, and what was the point of getting rich if you were too dead to spend it?

Randall sucked on his ice cube, stared at the rug and wondered why Gary Silk wanted a flashlight. He glanced up and caught Gary staring at him, went back to studying the carpet.

"Tell me about Moira," said Gary.

"Like what?"

"How'd you meet her?"

"I dunno." Randall rubbed his chin, inspected his nails. "At a club."

"Where was she, at the bar?"

Randall frowned, trying to remember. He shook his head. "No, not at the bar. It was at Lucy's, you know where that is?"

"Over on Haro, that the place?"

Randall nodded. "She was sitting at a table with a guy I knew. I went over and introduced myself. Turned out we had mutual friends. One thing led to another — you know how it is."

"She an addict at the time?"

"Light," said Randall. "Couple spoons a day."

"So what happened, you took her back to your place, jumped her bones . . ."

Randall grinned despite himself, remembering the moves he'd made.

"At the time, was she hooking?"

"Had a job at a radio station. Receptionist. Sat at the front desk and typed and answered the phone, shit like that."

"Rode the jockeys," said Gary. "When'd you start living together?"

"That first night she came over, she never left. I mean, she never went back to her apartment. It was near the end of the month and the rent was due, but I told her to forget it. She left all her clothes, the food that was in the fridge, her jewelry. I gave her money so she could buy a bunch of new stuff, replace what she'd lost. She quit her job."

"You bought her some flashy new clothes, put her out on the street?"

"It was the best thing for her, believe me. She was bored, sitting around the apartment. Also it was costing me a bundle, all the goddamn dope she was sticking into her body." It was hot in the den, but Randall held out his hands to the fire. "Besides, it was the thing she did best. She was a natural, why not take advantage?"

"You keep sleeping with her?" said Gary.

"Well, yeah. Sure."

"Weren't you afraid of . . . disease?"

"She was careful. Took precautions, know what I mean? All the time I was with her, the worst thing she caught was a cold."

"And you trusted her?"

"Trusted her?"

"In the sack."

Randall frowned.

"When you were doing it," said Gary, "did you believe her when she seemed to be enjoying herself. Or did you worry it might be an act, that she was faking it like she did on the street?"

"She never had to fake anything," said Randall. He thought about her for a moment, tried to remember exactly what she looked like. Orange hair streaked through with green, or was it blue? The pinhead diamond she liked to wear in her nose. Surprising how tough it was, to bring her back. "I already told you, she was a natural. Made that Xavier Hollander dame look like Mother Teresa."

"I wish I'd known her," said Gary. He smiled. "What you do with the body, by the way?"

Randall hadn't quite made up his mind about that. Moira was back at the apartment, waiting for him in the tub. He shrugged. "Nothing special."

Gary went over to the bookcase, selected a thin volume and opened it and took out a small map. "You ever see this?"

"What is it?"

"Map of the city, the suburbs. Shows you all the most popular places for ditching a body."

"Oh yeah?" Randall was interested. He put his empty glass down on the carpet beside his chair, leaned forward.

"Stanley Park gets most of the action," said Gary. "Makes sense, if you think about it. Convenient, right? Second most popular place is way over there in North Van, Mount Seymour Park. A long drive, but I guess it must be worth it. Ever been there?"

"No," said Randall. "Can't say I have."

Randall heard footsteps in the hall. Frank came into the room. He was wearing a brown leather jacket with a sheepskin collar and held a big five-cell flashlight in his right hand.

"What took you so long?" said Gary.

"I had to feed the cats." Frank gave Randall a wink. "Little furballs rub up against my leg, I can't resist it. Makes me melt like butter."

"You didn't give them that leftover chicken was on the bottom shelf of the fridge, I hope."

"Cat food," said Frank. "A tin each of Miss Mew, and a bowl of milk."

"Water's better for them."

"Better for you, too, Gary. But every time I look at you, you're drinking beer."

"Beer's got electrolytes. When you exercise the way I do, you got to replace your electrolytes. Can't get by without 'em, that's all there is to it."

Frank nodded, thinking *electrolytes*? What did Gary think he was, a fuckin' light bulb?

Gary folded the map and put it in the book between the last page and the cover, slid the book back into the bookcase. "Batteries okay?"

Frank switched the flashlight on, shone the beam into Randall's eyes and made him squint.

"Let's go," said Gary.

They went downstairs and through the huge gleaming kitchen, empty except for the quartet of Siamese cats and the muted gurgle of the dishwasher. Out the back door into the warmth of the late August evening. The sky was cloudy, dark. To their right there was a spacious brick patio surrounded on three sides by apple and plum trees; to their left the glass-enclosed walkway that led to the squash court. Frank led them down a path of interlocking pink brick, past a small fishpond towards the far end of the back yard.

"Where we going?" said Randall.

Frank hit him in the small of the back, sent him skittering down the path.

The property was about one hundred and fifty feet wide and almost four hundred feet deep — altogether a little less than three-quarters of an acre. With the house and outbuildings it was worth in the neighborhood of a couple of million dollars. There were always real estate agents pounding on the door. Gary invited the pretty ones in for a drink, fed them vodka martinis at ten in the morning. So far none of them had put out. Still, you never knew.

There was a narrow unpaved lane at the back of the yard, behind a six-foot high fence of rough-sawn cedar boards. The lane was dark, no streetlights. The beam of the flashlight swept across the fence and then held steady on what seemed to be a garden — long, orderly rows of slumping green plants.

"Wanna show you something," said Gary.

Frank grabbed Randall's arm. Randall saw that Gary had picked up a stick, no, a pitchfork. Randall's face was sticky and damp. A mosquito shrieked into his ear. He slapped himself on the side of the head. Frank led him off the path and across a patch of soft ground. He could smell the earth, moist and gluey. He stumbled and almost fell.

"Gimme the flash," said Gary. The beam of light wandered across the rows of plants and steadied on a fat green and orange striped squash.

"That my baby?" said Gary.

Frank crouched beside the squash, brushed away some mud, fingered a rectangle of cardboard attached to the stem of the plant by a short length of coarse brown twine. "Number sixteen?"

"Yeah, that's the one." Gary punched Randall on the shoulder. "Look at the size of that thing. Is that a goddamn squash or is that a goddamn squash?" He played the beam of light over the squash and then shone it into Randall's eyes.

"I thought they grew on trees," Randall said.

"Frank buries you here," said Gary, "the roots'll wrap around your bones and nobody'll ever find you." He stuck the pitchfork in the ground and then pulled it out again. Lumps of sticky black earth clung to the tines. Gary poked Randall in the belly. Randall didn't know what to do or say. He could feel the damp seeping up through the thin soles of his hundred-dollar Italian slip-ons.

"Keep looking for the dope dealer," said Gary. He threw away the pitchfork, passed the flashlight to Frank and started back towards the house.

Frank led Randall to the back gate. He swung the gate open and Randall followed the beam of the flashlight into the lane. The gate swung shut behind him. His car was parked out front. He was going to have to hoof it all the way down to the end of the lane and back up the street, half a mile or more.

It was pitch dark. No streetlights. No moon. Not a goddamn star in the sky. He started walking.

When Frank came back into the kitchen he found Gary crouched down in front of the fridge, ripping chunks of meat off the corpse of a cold chicken.

Gary glanced up, jaws working. "There's something I wanted to ask you, Frank."

"What's that?"

"The night we had Oscar Peel and Pat Nash over for a visit, you remember Peel knocked some of my trophies off the fireplace mantle and one of them broke?"

"Yeah, sure. Who could forget?"

"The base off one of them is missing. You know where it is, seen it around?"

Frank shook his head, no. "Is it important, Gary?"

"Probably the maid tossed it in the garbage. See if you can get the thing fixed, welded to a new base. Make it read 'First Place, Men's Singles, Inter-City Squash Championships 1988'."

"I thought you were runner-up that year."

"Just do it, okay?"

"Whatever you say, Gary."

Gary pushed himself to his feet, strolled out of the kitchen. He'd left the refrigerator door open, simply hadn't bothered to shut it. Where he'd been eating, the polished hardwood floor was littered with slivers of meat, yellow globules of fat. Frank shut the door and cleaned up the mess, fed the leftovers to the cats.

Summer was almost over, winter was on the way. But Frank knew that no matter what the season, as long as he stayed with Gary, the days would just keep on getting longer.

14

The deck of the Seabus shuddered beneath Paterson's feet as the 1600 BHP twin diesels were thrown into reverse. The ferry slowed abruptly, screws churning the water to a froth, and then the roar of the engines faded to a steady drone.

All he'd been able to think about during the twelve-minute ride across the harbor was that the man he'd shot probably had friends who'd be waiting for him when he got to the other side.

He peered anxiously into the purplish glare of the fluorescent lights. There were only three people, two men and a woman, waiting to board the Seabus for the run back to the city. The men were in their late twenties, both of them wearing jeans and black leather jackets. Under the lights their faces were unnaturally pale, eyes dark and hollow.

Once the ferry was underway, all passengers were locked inside until the electronically operated doors slid open at the end of the run. The vessel was designed so passengers boarded on the port side and disembarked on the starboard side. The system was fully automatic, impersonal but highly efficient.

Paterson moved towards the exit nearest the bow. Nobody paid any attention to him. He squeezed into the crowd. The automatic doors slid open. He pushed forward and hurried up the ramp towards the street, constantly twisting and turning to peer behind him.

Outside the terminal the landscape was dominated by huge elevated ramps supported by massive pillars of rough gray concrete. Beneath the ramps a strip of oil-stained asphalt was used by the municipal buses that connected with the ferry and serviced the North Shore.

A uniformed bus driver stood beside his vehicle, smoking a

cigarette. Paterson asked him for directions to the nearest taxi stand. The man dropped the stub of the cigarette on the asphalt, ground it under his heel and pointed over his shoulder towards a cab idling at the curb. Before Paterson could thank him he'd climbed into the bus and the door shut behind him with a hiss of compressed air.

The cab was a dark blue late-model Cadillac, the cabbie a middle-aged Italian who was bald except for a fringe of gray above his ears. He was wearing a dark blue suit, crisp white shirt, dark blue tie decorated with diagonal rows of little silver pigs.

Paterson climbed inside, shut the door. The taxi was showroom clean, smelled vaguely of peppermint.

The cabbie eyed him warily in the rearview mirror. Paterson pulled out his wallet, flashed a twenty. "Can you recommend a hotel?"

"The Wyndam's pretty good. A little pricey, maybe. But worth it."

"Let's go."

The Wyndam turned out to be a concrete highrise with rooms starting in the sixty-dollar range. Paterson used his Visa card, paid in advance for one night.

A bellboy with a Bob Hope nose and shiny black pants led him into the elevator and up to a room on the fifth floor. He unlocked the door with a flourish, handed Paterson the key and went over to the window and pulled the drapes on an uninspiring view of Marine Drive — an endless string of self-serve gas stations and used-car lots, take-out chicken and pizza joints. Gaily colored plastic flags flapped in the breeze. The hard scrawl of neon faded into the distance. The bellboy turned the TV on and off. He showed Paterson where the bathroom was, but not, surprise, how to flush the toilet. He loitered near the door. Paterson gave him a dollar, locked the door behind him.

The room was quiet except for the distant hum of traffic. He turned on the television and found himself watching a Mary Tyler Moore rerun. Ted's hairdresser had taken early retirement and was moving to Miami Beach. Ted was inconsolable.

He turned down the volume. The bulk of the heroin was still hidden on his sailboat, but he'd taken one of the half-pound bags with him, proof, if he needed it, that he was serious. The heroin, along with his expensive pigskin briefcase, had been left in the skid-road hotel room. The briefcase had a small brass plaque with his initials on it.

He worried about that for a while, and then let it go. He thought about the money. Tried not to think of all the pain and anguish and human suffering the heroin would cause. What it boiled down to was he'd shot a man so his wife could keep her microwave. The guy was a pimp and God knew what else, but so what? He might've killed him, and his actions were indefensible.

What if he went back down to Coal Harbor and tossed the rest of the heroin into the ocean? Then what? The price of a fix would skyrocket, but the junkies wouldn't go away. Nothing would change.

His first obligation was to his wife and kids. The bottom line was that his family depended on him. He had a standard of living to maintain.

And the goddamn plum-colored Porsche had absolutely nothing to do with it.

On the TV, Ted burst into tears and Mary put her arms around him, patted him on the back and rolled her eyes. Paterson turned the sound right off. He picked up the phone and dialled room service and ordered a hamburger and fries, coffee, a couple of double Scotches. What he needed was a hot shower and a stiff drink, a good night's sleep. Time to flush the adrenalin out of his system, clear his mind.

He'd tried to make a connection and it'd been a total disaster. Jesus, there were fractured moments when it all seemed like somebody else's idea of a nightmare — he couldn't quite believe he'd actually shot the bastard, pointed the Ruger at him and blasted away, pumped two or was it three rounds into the guy.

And that as he'd hurried up the ramp from the Seabus he'd been ready to shoot anybody who got in his way.

There had to be a better way of doing business. All he had to do was figure out what it was.

One thing for sure. It was too late to turn back now.

15

The phone on Eddy Orwell's desk rang twice and then fell silent. Orwell paused, hand hovering like a fat pink butterfly. Shrugged. Went back to his paperwork. The phone rang again. He snatched it up and said, "Jeez, Judith, I been trying to get ahold of you all goddamn mor . . ."

His beefy face flushed red.

"Hey, sorry. I thought . . . Yeah, sure. 'Course I got a pencil, go right ahead."

Orwell mashed the phone against his ear to drown out the clatter of a distant telex, scrawled an address on a pad and said thank you and goodbye and waited until the beat cop on the other end had disconnected, then slammed down the phone. Tore the sheet from the pad and folded the sheet in half and put it in his shirt pocket, pushed his chair away from his desk. Stood up. Checked to make sure the slip of paper hadn't fallen out of his pocket. Slung his sharkskin jacket over his broad and muscular shoulder, stomped the length of the squadroom and rested his narrow masculine hip against Parker's desk.

Orwell was wearing a pale blue short-sleeved shirt. The muscles of his arms flexed and bulged. Parker was punching the buttons of a pocket calculator, working out the monthly payments on a new Honda Civic. She glanced up, her eyes flat, incurious.

"Whatcha doin'?" said Orwell.

"My job," said Parker. "Why don't you go do yours?"

"Ouch," said Eddy. His head snapped sideways, as if he'd been punched. He gave Parker a doleful look, rubbed his jaw.

Parker ignored him.

"Where's Jack?" said Orwell.

"With Bradley."

Orwell put his hands on his hips and turned to stare at the door to Bradley's office. "So how come I don't hear anybody yelling?"

"Because they're both adults, Eddy, and adults don't always find it necessary to yell at each other to make a point."

"Yeah, sure." Orwell jerked a thumb at the calculator. "Working out your taxes?"

"My car's burning oil. It needs a new engine."

"The Volks?" Orwell mimed shock. "I thought those things ran forever. Remember that Woody Allen movie, *Sleeper*, where he's on the run from the cops and finds an old Beetle in a cave. Car's all covered in dust, it's been sitting there about two hundred years. He turns the key and it starts right up. You catch that movie?"

Parker nodded.

"Then he decides to get rid of it. Drives it off a cliff into a lake or whatever. Damn thing won't sink."

"Was there something you wanted, Eddy?"

"People laughed their heads off when Woody started that car," said Orwell. "Not me, though. Two hundred years old, Volkswagen or not, I guarantee that battery would've been dead as a doornail."

"A new engine is going to cost me almost a thousand dollars," said Parker.

"He's got a serious side, though. You see *Love and Death*?"

"But the upholstery's falling apart and . . ." Parker's voice trailed off. Orwell, clearly not listening, had taken a slip of paper from his shirt pocket and was squinting at it as if he was having trouble deciphering his own writing. "A hotel, the Vance. You know it?"

"Why?" said Parker.

"The desk clerk just phoned. He's got a body, room three-eighteen. Spears is still in bed with the mumps, clap, whatever he's got."

The door to Bradley's office swung open. Willows came out and started to walk towards them.

Orwell stepped away from Parker's desk. "So, since I'm all alone, I wondered if maybe you were interested in helping out?"

"Are you pulling my leg, Eddy?"

"Huh?" said Orwell, frowning.

Willows pointed at Orwell. "Bradley wants to see you, Eddy."

"What about?"

"He'll let you know."

Orwell held up the slip of paper. "I just got a call. A homicide."

"The Vance," said Parker. "Room three-eighteen."

Willows snatched the slip of paper from Orwell's hand. Orwell snatched it back.

"Eddy!" yelled Bradley from the far end of the squad room.

"When'd you get the call?" said Willows.

"Just a few minutes ago. Why?"

"There was a 'shots fired' report a couple of days ago," said Parker. "The responding officers found some blood, but that's about all."

"Think there might be a connection?" said Orwell.

Willows indicated the calculator. "Got a problem?"

"I'm trying to figure out," Parker said, "if I should get myself a new partner."

For a split second, Willows thought she was serious. He hoped like hell that moment didn't show.

There was a uniform down on the street, another on the landing, two more lounging inside the room. The desk clerk was standing in the hallway looking as if he was waiting in line to go to the bathroom. He was twenty-eight or maybe twenty-nine years old, very thin, about five foot six. He was wearing a black leather vest over a black shirt, black Levis. His face was like a wedge of Swiss cheese, flat and white and oily. A tiny diamond sparkled in his left ear. He had watery brown eyes and his teeth were stained the color of weak coffee by a lifetime of fifty-cent cigars. His posture was terrible.

"Somebody call the techs and ME?" said Willows.

One of the cops nodded. "Ten, maybe fifteen minutes ago."

The clerk ran his fingers through his hair. Parker noticed that his nails were painted pale blue.

"What's your name?" said Willows.

"Pete Blattner."

"When'd you find the body, Pete?"

"About half an hour ago. I dialled nine-eleven right away. We got strict rules."

"You touch anything?"

"Hey, I know better'n that."

"Didn't go through her pockets?"

"If she's broke, officer, it ain't my fault."

"Has anybody else been in this room that you know about?"

Blattner hesitated. "Well, yeah. Sure. Of course."

"Who?" said Parker.

"The fella rented it. Guy who told me about the dame in the first place."

"What's *his* name?"

"I got no idea. You want me to check the register?"

"Is he still in the hotel?" said Parker.

Pete Blattner jerked his thumb over his shoulder. He adjusted his suspenders. "He's across the hall, in room three-fifteen. Soon as he found out about the body, he came right back to the desk. Real disgusted. Wanted a different room or his money back."

"Seems reasonable," said the taller of the two cops leaning against the door.

"What I figured, especially since she's dead," said Blattner. He got up on his toes and tried to look over Claire Parker's shoulder at the body stretched out on the bed. Parker was too tall for him. He sank back, rocked on his heels. "She is dead, ain't she? I mean, not just unconscious."

"When was the room rented?"

"Night before last. There was a shooting in there a couple days ago. Room was sealed with crime tape . . ."

Willows nodded. Ident would seal the room and keep it that way until a blood analysis had been done.

"Who took the room, after you removed the tape?"

"I knew you'd ask me that, so I checked. Some guy named Smith. Mr John Smith."

"Was Mr Smith with anybody?"

"No, all alone. The rate's higher for two people. We don't allow guests before ten in the morning or after ten at night."

"When did Mr Smith vacate the room?"

"Beats me. Had to be sometime before eleven this morning.

Check out time's at eleven o'clock sharp. No loitering. Management's got a real strict policy. You try to stay late, I got orders to use my pass key, go in and kick your ass outta there."

"I'll try to remember that," said Willows.

Blattner laughed. He spat a shred of tobacco on the floor and said, "Whoops, sorry. Don't wanna fuck up your crime scene."

"What did Mr Smith look like?" said Parker.

"I already told the other cops, the ones that came a couple of days ago, after the shooting. You hear about that?"

"Describe him," said Willows.

Blattner gave him a reasonably accurate description of Randall DesMoines.

Willows wrote it all down in his notebook. He got Blattner's full name, his address. "We're going to want to talk to you again," he said.

"Meantime, don't leave town. Right?"

"Right."

"You want me, the first place you should try is probably the unemployment office. Way things have been going, I got a feeling I'm gonna get fired."

There was no bathroom. Willows knew there would be a communal one, at the end of the hall. It was part of the crime scene. He sent a uniformed cop down the hall to guard the door, told another cop to keep an eye on the second witness — the occupant of room three-fifteen.

The girl was lying on her back on the bed, her legs straight out in front of her and her arms at her sides, fists clenched. Willows went over to the bed and looked down at her.

"No purse," said Parker.

"How old would you say she was?"

"Nineteen, maybe twenty."

"Maybe she's lying on it. Or we've got ourselves a murder, and whoever killed her did it for money."

The girl was wearing glasses with oversized black plastic frames, a plain white blouse, pleated black skirt, black high-heeled shoes. Her legs were bare. No nylons, pantyhose or socks. Her hair was the color of a Mandarin orange, shot through with streaks of bright green. She wore no makeup, not even lipstick, but there was a small diamond on a pin stuck through her left nostril. Her skin was very pale. Except for the hair and the diamond, she could've worked in a bank or maybe a law office. Willows moved a little closer. He examined the clenched hands for evidence of defensive wounds, a weapon or perhaps a small bottle or vial that might have contained drugs or poison.

Nothing.

There was a thin gold chain around her neck, and a rectangular pendant with the name 'Moira' inscribed in block letters. Although it was the end of summer, there were no tan lines on her fingers to indicate she normally wore a ring. Her clothes were clean and freshly pressed. There was no visible evidence of blood or any other kind of stain.

"She looks as if she came straight from the dry cleaners," said the tall cop.

The girl's right eye was wide open. The left eye was shut. The eye that was open was dark green. The pupil was very small, a pinpoint of black.

"Kind of unusual," said Parker. "One eye open and the other eye shut."

"An open and shut case," said the cop.

Willows turned to him and said, "Why didn't I send you down the hall to guard the toilet, instead of your partner?"

"You ever see anything like that before?" Parker said.

"Never."

"Winking at us. As if it was a joke. You think she might've been left like that on purpose?"

"Let's not get ahead of ourselves," Willows said. He glanced up as the medical examiner came into the room. The ME's name was Bailey Rowland. He was physically nondescript but the detectives liked to call him 'Popeye' because of the pince-nez he wore when he was working. Popeye nodded at Willows and Parker. He approached the body, put his bag down on the floor beside the bed.

Willows pointed at the cop with the mouth. "Can you keep a timetable?"

The cop nodded. Willows was giving him the job of making a written record of all arrivals and departures; keeping track of who visited the crime scene, and when.

Willows began to write a description of the victim in his notebook. He recorded her sex, approximate age, eye and hair color, a detailed description of her clothing, the fact that there was no apparent cause of death. He noted the woman's general physique, asked Parker for an estimate of her height and weight.

Popeye had his rectal thermometer out. He shot his cuff and studied his watch. "The photographer going to get here sometime today, is he?"

"Any minute," said Parker. It was the ME's job to try to determine the apparent cause of death, and whether any observed injuries were ante or post-mortem. It was also his job to determine the approximate time of death, as indicated by body temperature, lividity, the presence of rigor mortis and various other signs. But no matter how busy he was, no exceptions, the ME couldn't go to work until the crime scene in its original condition had been thoroughly sketched and photographed.

Willows finished with his observations and began to draw the scene. The demands on his limited talent were not all that great. The room was rectangular. He paced it off and found it was about ten feet wide by twelve deep. There was a cold-water sink to the left of the door. The only furniture in the room was the bed and a battered oak veneer bureau. He sketched the bureau first and then the bed, complete with body.

The corpse was so neatly laid out that it looked ridiculous, child-like in its simplicity of posture. He noted the location of the solitary window, decided it would be impossible for anyone outside to see into the room. When he was finished, he went over his notes to make sure he hadn't missed anything the first time around.

Popeye was checking his watch for about the hundredth time when Mel Dutton breezed into the room. Dutton said hello to Willows, apologized for keeping Popeye waiting, smiled at Parker. Dutton was short and bald. He had reached the age where his metabolism had slowed and he was gaining weight so fast that he had to constantly replace his clothes, so that lately he'd seemed very well dressed, for a cop. Today he was wearing a pearl gray pinstripe suit, black cowboy boots with silver-tipped toes and four-inch heels. In the boots, his eyes were almost on a level with Parker's.

Dutton unslung his Nikon, peered down at the body through the viewfinder. "Mind moving off to the side, doc?"

The power winder of the Nikon whirred and clicked. Dutton danced lightly around the room. "Can I pull that curtain?" he said to Parker.

"Leave it," said Willows.

"The light'd be a whole lot better," Dutton said to Parker. "Bright enough so I wouldn't have to use the flash. Might get something interesting."

"Maybe later," said Willows. Dutton was a bachelor. He had a lot of spare time and his hobby was photography. Willows had been to his apartment once. Dutton had converted the bathroom into a darkroom. He spent every spare dime he had on supplies and equipment, and had subscriptions to dozens of glossy photography magazines. He was always entering contests. Taking pictures was all he ever wanted to talk about, the only subject that could hold his interest.

Dutton switched to his Polaroid. Waltzing around the room, contorting his body into weird shapes, crouching and stretching, he quickly shot two packs of film; one color and one black and white. As the developing film was ejected from the camera he held the shots pinched between his pudgy fingers like a deck of oversized cards. "That it?" he said when he was finished.

"If you're happy," Parker said.

"The curtain?"

"Maybe next time."

"I want a pack of unexposed Polaroid film, Mel," said Willows.

"What for?" Confusion and then suspicion dominated Dutton's beefy face.

"Official police business," said Willows, grinning.

Dutton reluctantly gave him the film. He shuffled slowly towards the door. "I'll send up the thirty-five mil stuff as soon as it's ready."

"The sooner the better," said Willows. His stock response.

"Can I go to work now?" said Popeye.

"Let's wait for the techs," said Willows. "I want to dust some skin, see if we can pick up any of Mr Smith's latents."

"That why you want the film?"

Willows nodded.

Popeye looked at his watch, which was solid gold and showed the phases of the moon. Very convenient, if you happened to be a werewolf. Or just a normal human being who liked to know when to go crazy. "Quarter past one," said Popeye. "No wonder I'm hungry. There by any chance a decent restaurant around here?"

"The Red Hawk Cafe," said Parker. "Halfway down the block, same side of the street. They've got a big neon sign hangs out over the sidewalk, you can't miss it."

"Half an hour," said Popeye. "You need me, come and get me."

Willows nodded. There was something under the bed. He got down on his hands and knees. A hypodermic, plunger all the way down, barrel empty. And a spent cartridge. Small, .22 or .25 calibre. He tried to remember if Dutton had taken any shots of the underside of the bed. He was pretty sure he had—the flash would catch the casing. He noted the location in his sketch, then folded an evidence bag over his hand like an outsized mitten and picked up the hypo, used another bag to retrieve the spent shell. A .22 Long Rifle. Not a .25. So much for coincidence.

The cop at the door noted in his timetable that the tech arrived at twenty-seven minutes past one. The tech's name was Tim Fisher. He was about six feet tall, a hundred eighty pounds, and he was wearing a drab brown sports jacket and drab brown trousers. His heavy brown shoes had sturdy rubber heels and thick leather soles. He nodded at Willows and Parker and said, "What've you got, Jack?"

Willows shrugged. "Not much. There was a hypo and a spent cartridge under the bed."

"Shot or shot up," said Fisher. "Makes no difference to me, as long as she's dead."

"There's a communal bathroom down at the end of the hall," Willows said. "We're going to get a lot of wild prints, but . . ."

Fisher nodded. He'd been there before.

"She didn't rent the room," said Willows. "A guy by the name of Smith signed the register. Could be she died somewhere else, Smith dragged her up here and dumped her. I want you to try to pick some latents off her skin."

"Sure," said Fisher.

"Mel Dutton gave me a pack of Polaroid film, if you need it."

Fisher shook his head. "I've got some Kromekote cards. Use the film to take some pictures of your wife and kids." Willows gave Fisher a sour look, but Fisher missed it. Parker took an involuntary step towards Willows. He glanced sharply at her, his face pale, mouth drawn tight. She stood motionless. Fisher put his briefcase down on the floor and popped it open. "I better do the latents first, Jack."

"Whatever."

Kromekote cards are similar to photographic paper, but with a very high gloss. To transfer a latent print from human flesh, the card is placed on the skin where it's assumed a latent may be located. A firm, even pressure is applied to the card for a period of roughly three seconds. The card is then lifted from the skin and dusted with ordinary black fingerprint powder. Any prints that are successfully retrieved will be a mirror image of a normal print and must be reversed in the photographer's darkroom.

Fisher used a total of fourteen of the five by seven inch cards. He searched for prints on the dead girl's neck, the area directly behind her ears and ear lobes, and her wrists. Because there was a possibility the body might have been dragged or carried from a different location, he also applied cards to her heels and the skin around her ankles. He lifted her skirt. No panties. He pressed cards against the flesh of both thighs. As he finished with each card, he dusted it down and then put it into a pre-marked evidence envelope. As he dusted the last of the cards, he glanced up at Willows, shrugged.

"Check the bedframe and windowsill," Willows said. "We'll let the ME go over her and then I want to take off her blouse, try the area around her upper arms and breasts."

"If you say so," said Fisher without enthusiasm.

Latent prints on living flesh maintain their integrity for a maximum of approximately ninety minutes. On a corpse, survival time depends on a number of complex factors, primarily atmospheric conditions and the state of the skin. The Kromekote lift technique was new to Fisher, and it was obvious he didn't have much faith in it. But he'd do his job, and that was all Willows cared about.

Willows told the cop at the door to hustle over to the Red Hawk Cafe and retrieve the medical examiner.

There were no plastic or visible or latent prints on the bed or windowsill or bureau, none on the lightswitch or wall in the area of the lightswitch.

The doorknob yielded a partial palm, three fingers and a thumb. Willows was fairly certain the prints were useless; that the occupant of room three-fifteen would provide a perfect match.

Fisher went down the hall to the bathroom. He dusted the bathroom door and the doorknob and found that both were covered in fingerprints, dozens of them, layer upon layer. The bathroom was small, with a sink and toilet, no tub. Fisher dusted down the inside of the door, and then the lightswitch and wall around the switch. He went to work on the sink and taps, the surrounding wall area, then slipped on a pair of disposable rubber gloves and dusted the cracked plastic toilet seat, the water tank, flush handle. When he was finished he had hundreds of overlaps and dozens of partials, maybe a total of twenty useful prints. Because there was always a possibility that a print could be damaged during the attempt to lift it, he shot the worthwhile prints with the lab's Polaroid CU-5 fixed-focus camera.

He was taking the last of the Polaroids when Willows showed up.

"Let's do the rest of the Kromekotes, Tim."

"The ME finished already?"

Willows didn't see much point in telling Fisher that the uniform he'd sent down to the Red Hawk Cafe had found Popeye curled up in a fetal position on the floor by his table, drenched in tears and vomit, suffering from a severe case of food-poisoning. By now he'd be in St Paul's, getting his stomach pumped. A replacement ME was on the way but wasn't expected for at least another hour. By the time he reached the crime scene it was probable that any latents in the area of the victim's shoulders and breasts would have melted into her skin.

It had been a long day. Before it was over, it was going to get a whole lot longer.

16

Frank was halfway into his chair when the waiter arrived at the table. Frank grabbed him by the elbow, said, "Whatcha got on tap?"

"Miller Lite . . . Labatts . . ." The waiter frowned, trying to remember. "We got another one, what is it . . ."

"Gimme a Labatts," said Frank. "A pint. What's your bar rye?"

"Double Crown."

"Make it a Seagrams."

"Seagrams, you got it."

Frank smiled, gave the arm a squeeze, let go. The waiter was all dolled up in the house uniform of a big white cowboy hat, shiny black fringed pants and a crisp white shirt. The shirtsleeve was rumpled and creased where Frank had held him, and there were dark sweat rings under his armpits. His shift had started ten minutes ago, but as he retreated towards the bar he looked as if he'd just finished a long, hard ride.

"Jesus," said Pat Nash, grinning. "You scared the hell out of him."

"Did I?"

"See the look on his face? Like he just sat on one of Gary's cactuses."

Frank rolled his shoulders, a careless shrug. In his life, he'd found that frightening people wasn't usually a bad thing to do. He glanced across the table at Nash, who was drinking Granville Island Lager out of a longneck bottle. Frank wondered about that. He'd have thought the beer was a little upscale for Nash, and it was in the back of his mind that a bottle, because it was heavier and easier to handle, made a better weapon than a glass.

Did Nash have something in mind, or was he just being careful? Frank had killed Oscar Peel, and Oscar and Nash were distantly related. Most families weren't all that close, but some were. He leaned across the table, looked Nash straight in the eye, and said, "How you feel about Oscar?"

Nash didn't hesitate. "He was a jerk. Tell you the truth, Tracy's better off without him."

The waiter came back with a shot glass full of rye and a dimpled pint mug, his ten-gallon hat casting the table in shadow. Frank drank an inch of beer and then dropped the rye, shot glass and all, into the pint and drained the whole thing down. He licked his lips and waved his hand at the table. "Bring us another round, pard. And half a dozen pickled eggs and a couple packs of pretzels."

The waiter jerked his thumb over his shoulder, down towards the dimly lit rear of the bar. "Pretzels in the machine down there by the pool tables. Need some change?"

"No," said Frank. "You do."

Frank waited until the guy had turned his back and then let Nash have a look at his new gun, a Magnum Research Desert Eagle .44 calibre semi-auto gas operated blaster with a fourteen-inch barrel. The weapon was almost two feet long, including the home-made noise suppressor that Frank had let Gary take down to the basement and paint matt-black with a spray can from the local Home Hardware store. Put wheels on it, the damn thing was almost as big as a tank. Frank figured the silencer was good for maybe five or ten shots before the baffles gave out. He lowered the gun under the table and held it between his wide-spread legs with the hard length of the barrel pressed up against the inside of Nash's thigh. When Nash's eyes were as big as they were going to get, Frank said, "Gary's kind of disappointed in you, Pat. Way he sees it, he gave you some time and you been pissing it away."

Pat Nash wanted to look around, see if anybody was watching. But he was afraid that if he lost eye contact with Frank, that Frank might squeeze the trigger. Dump like this he could empty the clip, knock back a couple more beers and *then* make his getaway. No hurry at all.

"Want to know what Gary said, exactly? 'Splash the bastard.'" Frank grinned. "Sure can turn a phrase, can't he?"

Nash drank some Granville Island Lager. The bottle thumped down on the table. Nash didn't let go of it, held on tight.

"Rub me out, huh."

"Kill you dead."

"You sure, Frank? I mean, maybe you didn't hear him right. It was nap time or something. Little dink had his mouth full of animal crackers and warm milk."

Frank threw back his head and cackled at the ceiling. His teeth looked like sugar cubes, unnaturally white and square.

"So what're you gonna do?" Nash said. He lifted the beer bottle to his lips and Frank tensed, but all he did was drink some beer.

Frank dug the blunt nose of the noise suppressor into the soft meat of Nash's thigh. "I do exactly what I'm told. Unless I feel like doing something entirely different. In which case I do that."

Pat Nash leaned back in his chair and waited. He wasn't sure, but he thought Frank was probably having a little fun with him. The waiter ambled over with another Granville Island Lager, Frank's beer and shot, a plastic bowl full of foul-smelling eggs, the pretzels. Coming towards them, he sounded like a reindeer. Nash looked down and saw the poor sap was wearing spurs as big around as the hubcaps on the old Pontiac that Oscar had died in. Jesus, what happened to the good old days, when a bar was a place you went to get drunk? The waiter put Frank's drinks and the eggs and pretzels down first, then Nash's beer. Frank gave him a twenty, waved away the change. Wasted money. Guy was so spooked he probably would've paid for the round, if Frank had asked him.

"Thing is," Frank said, "I liked the way you handled yourself the night we had to shoot Oscar. And I figure, why waste talent? Gary, on the other hand, his favorite thing is getting even with people. I saw a woman beat him to a parking space once, over at Oakridge, that big shopping mall? Gary waited three hours in the rain and then followed her home. She was driving a BMW 325CSi. Brand new. Fucking expensive car. Gary poured five gallons of diesel all over it, lit up with my Zippo, which I never got back."

Frank ate an egg, popped it into his mouth whole, chewed twice and swallowed.

"I had that Zippo eight years. Got it down in New Orleans. It was so old the chrome was all worn off. You know how hard it is not to lose a Zippo? Something about those lighters, I don't know what it is. Impossible to hold on to, they just disappear."

Frank ate another egg. Nash studied the bubbles rising in his beer.

"Gary burned that goddamn BMW to the ground. Came home and watched TV until three o'clock in the morning and then gave her a call. Told her if she ever tried anything like that again he'd sneak into her house a year or so down the road, inject strychnine into every piece of meat in the fridge, slaughter her whole goddamn family. Wipe 'em all out. The dog too, if she had one. And you know something? He meant every word of it, the dummy."

Nash reached across the table and picked up a bag of pretzels, squeezed until the air inside made the bag pop open. "Why are you telling me all this shit?" he said.

"Guy got shot up pretty good at the Vance. Randy DesMoines, you know him?"

"Don't think so," said Nash.

"Fella who splashed him said he found twenty keys of smack, needs some cash. Randy made a grab for the ring and got it stuffed up his ass. Shooter's gone for now but he'll be back. And the word is out, Gary's the man to see. What comes around, goes around, right? Gary's real eager to set up a meet. Get his drugs back and blow the fucker's head off."

"You want me to do the shooting," said Nash, and bit into his pretzel to hide his relief.

"That's right, only while you're at it, I want you to waste Gary, too." Frank paused, letting it sink in. "Then you and me can do a split. Percentages, I figure eighty my end and twenty for you. Sound good?"

Nash nodded, liking the idea a whole lot. The trick would be to do Gary and at the same time keep an eye on Frank, because although Frank seemed straight enough, he had an idea Frank wasn't the sharing kind.

Still, his style had always been to take things one step at a time, slow and easy.

He helped himself to another pretzel. Frank smiled at him. He chewed, swallowed, smiled back. Frank reached out and grabbed his third pickled egg, popped it whole into his mouth. His cheeks bulged. He drank some beer, swallowed. Burped. Scooped up another egg. Waved his hand at the bowl.

"Dig in, don't be shy."

"Thanks anyway, Frank." Nash watched Frank's jaws rise and fall. Gulp. Another mouthful of beer, a fifth egg. Nash sipped at his lager and kept his face blank. It was a weird situation, sitting there watching Frank stuff his face. Like he was watching a condemned man eat his last meal.

Because what was on his mind was Frank's store-bought teeth, how they'd crumble and splinter when he took his cannon away from him and used it to pistol-whip the shit out of him, just before he shot him dead.

17

The tide was on the ebb, and the swiftly-moving water, pushed by a fitful offshore breeze, was pale green and choppy, flecked with white.

Willows stood on the dock with his hands in his pockets and his back to the weather. Parker and a Marine Squad sergeant named Curtis were standing about twenty feet away. Despite the distance and the fact that they were downwind, Willows heard every word of the sergeant's argument as he tried to convince Parker the smart thing to do was not to come along for the ride.

"Never seen a floater, have you?"

"Not yet," said Parker.

Curtis had thick black hair combed straight back, a neatly trimmed salt-and-pepper moustache. His dark gray eyes were very calm. "It's not a pretty sight, young lady."

A detective is equal in rank to a corporal. Parker was outranked. She chose her words carefully. "It's my case and I'm going to stick with it. That's what I've been trained to do, sergeant. So why don't we just leave it at that."

Curtis glanced at Willows, who studiously ignored him. He turned back to Parker and said, "The head's belowdecks on your right. We just scrubbed the deck."

The body had been found in False Creek, fouled in the web of pilings of the huge wharf that supported the Granville Island Farmer's Market. Granville Island is not really an island at all, but simply a fat isthmus of land that had once been an industrial site but was now primarily a mix of parkland, speciality shops, restaurants and theatres. The man who'd found the corpse had been fishing for crab. He'd had the presence of mind to note the slashed throat. The indication of foul play had resulted in a call to

Major Crimes. Willows and Parker and Curtis were waiting at the Marine Squad's Coal Harbor base for VPD 98, the squad's thirty-one foot Uniflite, to pick them up.

Parker moved down the wharf towards Willows. The wind tore at her hair.

"Bit of a chauvinist, the sergeant."

Willows smiled. "He gave me the same speech, my first time out. Word for word, as a matter of fact."

"He called you a young lady?"

"No, he called me a young man. And I was, believe it or not." Willows turned up the collar of his black leather jacket. "Curtis has been around a long time, Claire. Remembering my first time out on the boat, I'd give you the same advice." Willows grinned. "That is, if I thought for a minute you might take it."

They heard the deep throb of the engines first, and then the boat came into view, crawling along at five knots to minimize its wake. Parker moved away from the edge of the wharf as the constable behind the wheel swung the boat around, inched closer to the dock.

"Lovely vessel, isn't she?" Curtis said to Parker. "Thirty-one feet in length, a ten-foot, six-inch beam. Walk-through transom, swim grid. She's powered by a pair of four hundred and forty horsepower Chrysler V-8 marine engines. Top speed of about thirty-five knots. But we won't be pushing it, not today."

Curtis stepped aboard and offered Parker his hand. She ignored him. He winked at Willows. VPD 98 had a crew of two constables. Both men were dressed in dark blue nylon floater jackets, regulation pants and baseball caps. The seahorse logo on the jackets was incongruous with the police crests high up on the jacket sleeves. The constable behind the wheel, Hollis, had regulation shoes but the second man was wearing black Reeboks, white sports socks. Willows had seen him around. He tried to remember his name. Leyton.

"Cast off," said Curtis. He glanced at his watch. Twenty past ten. Coal Harbor was a cul-de-sac. They'd have to cruise all the way around Stanley Park and up English Bay, beneath the

Burrard and Granville Street bridges. The trip would take at least twenty minutes.

"More comfortable inside," Leyton said to Willows.

It was crowded down below. Curtis sat in a padded blue bucket seat that looked as if it had been stripped from a sports car. Hollis sat in an identical chair. He wrote a few lines in the ship's log, a small, dark green, hardbound book, then put the log to one side and slowly eased the throttles forward. A bell rang shrilly.

"Oil pressure," said Curtis. The clanging of the bell stopped abruptly. The noise of the engines deepened and the bow rose slightly. Behind the control console there was a small Formica table and a narrow bench seat. Leyton asked Parker if she'd like to sit down. She said she preferred to stand. Leyton glanced at Willows, and then made himself comfortable.

They cruised past the Royal Vancouver Yacht Club and Deadman's Island, an Indian burial ground now used as a naval facility. Curtis passed out small white envelopes. To Parker he said, "Earplugs. We use them whenever engine revs exceed twenty-two hundred r.p.m. Union regulations."

The throttles were pushed all the way forward. The boat crashed into the sea. The earplugs were made of little tubes of white foam. Parker watched Curtis roll the foam between his finger and thumb, compressing it, then insert the plug into his ear and hold it in place while the foam expanded. She followed his lead.

Willows saw a freighter from Vladivostock. Sleek, shiny black cormorants preening themselves on a buoy. A raft of buffleheads, small black and white ducks locally called 'killer whale' ducks. Off to starboard, a twin-engine floatplane thundered past at an altitude of no more than a hundred feet, wings flashing bright yellow as it sideslipped towards the air terminal on the south shore of the harbor.

They rounded Hallelujah Point, the bronze statue of Harry Jerome, the Nine O'Clock Gun. The cannon had once signalled the end of the day to fishermen in English Bay. On one occasion a prankster had loaded it with a rock the size of a bowling ball, and blown a hole in the floating Shell gasoline station.

"How fast are we going?" Willows said to Leyton. He had to yell, because of the earplugs.

"About twenty-five knots. We can go faster, but only for short bursts. Too hard on the engines."

Off to Willows' left was Brockton Point, a favorite parking spot for night-time lovers. The path along the seawall was busy with cyclists and joggers, even the odd pedestrian who was content merely to walk. All around them the water sparkled in the sunlight. The wind was in their face now, but the tide was speeding them along and they were doing almost twenty knots. They passed beneath Lion's Gate Bridge, the cars and trucks and buses high above them seeming no larger than a child's toys.

There was traffic from two radios; a ship-to-shore unit and a Motorola that broadcast the regular police band. Willows noticed that the boat was also equipped with an MRDS, or Mobile Radio Dispatch System. The value of the unit was that it transmitted data on a miniature TV screen, effectively preventing the interception of information by radio and television reporters. Willows knew there would already be camera crews on the scene. If there had been foul play, there'd be footage of the body's recovery on the six o'clock news. If it was a suicide, the public would never find out about it.

The water off Spanish Banks was crowded with sails. The sergeant brought up his binoculars. "Lasers," he said. "The different clubs at Jericho get together, set up a figure-eight course."

Parker thought about the slim, graceful hulls cutting across the surface of the water. She thought about the body caught below. And found herself wondering, how many corpses, in all the seven seas? It didn't pay to think about it. A flock of crows swirled like dead leaves high above a copse of maple trees in Vanier Park. The bow of VPD 98 dropped as the revs were cut back. Curtis removed his earplugs. They cruised slowly past the Civic Marina and Coast Guard wharf, beneath the Burrard Street Bridge, dull thunder of traffic. Parker went out on deck.

A deep-sea tug slipped past. For a moment the two boats were very close. A seaman waved at them, but no one waved back. The wake of the tug made the Uniflite sway vigorously. Willows gripped the back of Curtis' chair.

Hollis turned the boat towards the small dock at Granville Island. The dock was used primarily by a fleet of small, electrically powered ferries that catered to people out for a short pleasure ride, or who wanted, for one reason or another, to approach the Island by water.

Constable Leyton went out on deck to attend to the mooring.

"Can you give me a hand with the stretcher?" Curtis asked.

Willows followed him to the bow of the boat. The stretcher was about six feet long and perhaps twenty inches wide, galvanized wire on a frame of half-inch metal tubing. There was a varnished slab of plywood for the body to lie on, a sort of rudder made of wood to keep the corpse's legs apart. The stretcher was held in place against the hull by two short lengths of nylon rope and two bands of thick black rubber. The sergeant worked on one end, Willows on the other.

"Smell anything?"

Willows sniffed the air, shook his head.

"It's been a couple of months since the last one, so I guess it's faded. But it's the worst stench on earth, believe me. Gets into your hair, your clothes. It's a nice tour, the Marine Squad. Until we have to pull one out of the water."

They lifted the stretcher off its brackets. Curtis flipped open the lid of a white-painted box. He removed a pair of surgeon's masks. "Think you can handle the stretcher, Jack?"

"Sure." Willows braced himself against the thin fiberglass hull. He could feel the gentle motion of the boat, the coolness of the water against the palm of his hand.

The sergeant removed a pair of disposable surgeon's gloves from a cardboard box fastened to the bulkhead. He pulled on the fragile gloves and then put on another pair of gloves, made of thick black rubber. The gloves and surgeon's mask were considered a necessary precaution. No one jumped off a bridge unless he had a reason. The threat of AIDS was always present.

They tied the stern of VPD 98 to the western end of the wharf, the bow to one of the pilings. Up on the dock, there was an unmarked Body Removal station wagon, a squad car and two uniformed policemen to keep the crowds away. The fisherman was waiting for them. He pointed out the location of the body, caught beneath about five feet of water.

Curtis took the man's name and address and telephone number, gave him one of his cards and sent him on his way. Let a civilian get a peek at what they were about to pull out of the water, next thing you knew you had a lawsuit on your hands.

Willows peered into the depths. He became aware of Parker standing beside him, leaning over the rail.

"What's he caught up on?" Curtis said to Leyton.

"Beats me, sergeant. Want me to fish him out?"

"In one piece," said Curtis.

Leyton slid an aluminum pike pole into the water. He used the piling for leverage. The body drifted away from the piling and then back again. All Willows could see was a vague, pale shape. The light was uncertain, like dusk on a dull and cloudy day. Leyton got a fresh grip on the pike pole. The aluminum bent in a graceful arc as he put his back into it. The body slipped away from the piling and then returned to embrace it once again.

"Jacket's caught on something." Leyton used the pike to stab at the water.

Parker heard the snap of rubber. Hollis was busy with the surgeon's gloves.

"Got him." There was a note of triumph in Leyton's voice, as if he'd hooked a particularly large fish.

The body rose swiftly towards the surface. Willows held the stretcher.

"Roll him over."

The man was wearing jeans and a bright yellow rain slicker. Leyton and Hollis slid the body on to the swim grid. The throat looked as if it had been slashed, but Willows knew it was the soft tissue that went first, so you couldn't be sure. Behind him, the door to the Uniflite's head slammed shut. He looked for Parker but couldn't find her.

Curtis started taking pictures. He'd been right about the body; it smelled like nothing else on earth.

It wasn't until they'd eased the corpse into the stretcher that Willows saw the wide overlapping bands of clear plastic tape over the mouth. The tape had lost much of its viscosity, was unravelling. He stared across the water. It was on the far side of the bridge, less than a quarter of a mile away, that they'd found the bloody shot-up Pontiac and the heel marks in the gravel leading down to the water.

He wondered how quickly he could get the coroner's office to do the autopsy, file the report. Goldstein had hair, he had blood. There was a chance the .25 calibre bullet was in there somewhere. If they could match it to the spent casing . . .

Parker came back on deck. She stared at the body, glanced across the water towards the bridge. "Think there might be a connection?"

"Wouldn't it be nice," said Willows.

Curtis and Leyton got down on the swim grid, unrolled a yellow bodybag of rubberized canvas. They were both wearing gloves and masks. The body shifted fitfully in the chop. Curtis held his breath, got a grip beneath the armpits.

Something was bothering Parker but she couldn't think what it was. She glanced up, towards the endless stream of traffic that hummed a dirge on the bridge.

"You okay?" said Curtis.

Parker nodded, but she wasn't so sure.

The air smelled clean and pure and the sky all above her was a rich, flawless blue. And that was it — what was on her mind. The weather was all wrong.

A day like this, it should have been raining.

18

The city morgue is on Cordova Street, conveniently located just around the corner from 312 Main. With its arched doorway and facade of orange brick highlighted by orderly rows of white-painted mullioned windows, the morgue remains an attractive building despite its grim function and the years of accumulated dust that lay upon it like a shroud.

The morgue's front entrance — the door used by the living — is painted bright red. Parker pushed the door open and stepped aside.

"Thank you," said Willows.

"My pleasure."

Parker pressed the elevator button, but Willows had already started up the stairs.

They reached the third floor and walked down a long, wide, brightly-lit corridor. This time Willows got the door. They entered the operating theatre, a large, square room with a floor of glossy blue tiles, walls that were lined from floor to ceiling with the refrigerated stainless steel drawers that serve as temporary coffins for the permanently down and out.

In the center of the room, a pair of zinc tables stood directly beneath a huge industrial skylight made of cast-iron and frosted glass. The tables were exactly thirty-six inches wide and seven feet long.

A corpse lay on the nearest of the tables; Willows went over and flipped back the sheet. A girl with bright blue eyes and color-coordinated hair shaved within an inch of her skull stared up at him.

The pathologist, a short, dark man named Brahms, turned away from the sink. "You wouldn't believe what happened to her," he said to Parker.

"Then there isn't much point in telling me about it," Parker replied.

Willows flipped the nylon sheet back over the corpse. He eyed the rows of stainless steel drawers. "Where's my floater?"

Brahms turned back to the sink, yanked a handful of paper towels from the dispenser. "We did the preliminary this morning. Finished a couple of hours ago." He dried his hands, tossed the used towels overhand into a metal wastebasket beneath the sink. "The report'll be on your desk by tomorrow morning. Want the highlights?"

"Please." Willows took out his notebook, flipped it open to a fresh page, tried to write down the date and discovered that his pen was out of ink.

Parker fished through her purse, found a Bic.

Brahms cleared his throat. "Your victim was shot at least four times, minimum of two weapons. He was hit once in the thigh, once in the gluteus maximus, a.k.a. ass, and twice in the head. Both head shots struck him in the left temple and exited above the right ear. The one he caught in the ass hit the femur at a sharp angle and lodged in the knee joint. That bullet and the one that got him in the leg were recovered and have been sent to the lab. At least two weapons were used. The one from the thigh was small-calibre. The round I dug out of his knee is probably from a three fifty-seven Magnum or a forty-five. Big, a cannon."

"He was dead when he went into the water?"

"You betcha. Either head shot would've killed him instantly."

"What condition were the bullets in?"

"The one that hit him in the thigh was in excellent shape. The second bullet was pretty banged up, but I'd say you should be able to make a comparison. Why, you got a gun?"

"Not yet," said Willows.

"This was the shooting that took place down by the Granville Street Bridge last weekend?"

Willows nodded.

"You didn't find anything in the car?"

"A hole in the roof."

“The hair was badly burned. A searing effect was noted. We found evidence of stippling.” Brahms glanced at Parker, as if unsure that she knew what he was talking about.

Stippling was an effect of shooting at point-blank range; pinpoint hemorrhaging due to unburned powder and metal shavings being driven into the victim’s flesh.

Parker was watching Willows take notes, the knuckles of his right hand white with pressure as he wielded her Bic pen. Willows stopped writing. He looked up. “What else?”

“The body was in pretty good shape, considering. At a depth of five or six feet the temperature of the water around here doesn’t change much, it’s fairly cold all year round.”

“Alcohol?”

“His blood level was point five. He’d had a few, but he was sober.”

“Fingerprints?”

Brahms shrugged. “The left hand was pretty bad, some kind of marine life had made a meal of it. The right hand was better, most of the skin was intact even though there was a lot of wrinkling.” He grinned. “You ever spend a couple of days soaking in the tub, you’ll know what I’m talking about.”

“My line of work, I’ve never felt that dirty.”

Brahms frowned. “To get a decent print, what we had to do was tie a string around the end of the thumb and fingers close to the knuckle joint, then use a hypo to inject water under the skin, fill out the finger. Ever seen it done?”

Willows shook his head.

“Tricky,” said Brahms. “One of your techs rolled the prints. Guy named Saunders. Mel Dutton was with him. Set up some lights and snapped a couple rolls.”

“What time was that?”

“Maybe an hour ago, little less. He’s putting on weight, Dutton. Looks a little older every time I see him.”

Willows handed the Bic back to Claire Parker.

“One more thing,” said Brahms. “The victim’s palate and tongue were badly lacerated, as if he’d had a sharp chunk of metal in his mouth, or maybe been punched.”

“Find anything?”

Brahms shook his head. "The mouth had been taped shut, but the tape came loose in the water."

Out on the street, as they walked back to 312 Main, Parker took a deep breath, filled her lungs with air. The mix of exhaust fumes and windblown grit seemed comparatively refreshing, after the cold and clammy atmosphere of the morgue.

Dutton had left a memo taped to Willows' telephone. He'd had a problem with the prints and he and Saunders had taken them to the more sophisticated facilities at the Coordinated Law Enforcement Unit on West Seventh.

Willows phoned CLEU. Saunders had come and gone. He tried Mel Dutton's number. No answer. Eddy Orwell and Farley Spears wandered into the squadroom. Spears held a handkerchief to his nose. Orwell was drinking a diet Pepsi. Spears sneezed, loudly blew his nose. Orwell saw Parker and ambled over to her desk.

"Hear you finally got a victim, that shooting down by the bridge."

Parker picked up her phone, started dialling.

Farley Spears sneezed again.

Orwell drank some Pepsi, jerked a thumb at Spears. "Guy waits until he's infectious, *then* he comes back to work."

Parker gave Orwell a look, as if he was something she'd found swimming around in her drink. He gave the Pepsi can a squeeze and wandered down to his desk at the far end of the squadroom. Spears said something to him. He glanced over his shoulder at Willows, as if worried about being overheard.

After a few minutes, Orwell and Spears approached Parker.

"What is it, Eddy?"

"Mel told us a couple slugs were recovered from the body, and one of them was from a forty-five."

"So?"

"There's a guy in the interrogation room, a chartered accountant. Picked him up about twenty minutes ago. Got a call from the White Spot on Georgia. Guy opened his briefcase to get his newspaper, waitress noticed he had a gun."

"Jack," said Parker.

Willows looked up from his desk. Parker motioned him over.

"Picked up a chartered accountant with a forty-five calibre Colt stainless," said Orwell. "Thing is, the guy claims he found the gun in the can at a nightclub over on Richards."

"When?" said Willows.

"Last Saturday night," said Orwell. "Think there might be a connection? Wanna talk to him?"

"Where's the Colt?"

"Lab's got it."

"Good work, Eddy."

The phone on Willows' desk started ringing. It was Mel Dutton. He told Willows that the floater had been identified; his name was Oscar Peel. Dutton had Peel's address, if Willows was interested.

"Bless you," Willows said.

Spears hadn't even been thinking about sneezing. He gave Willows a bewildered look.

"Let's go," Willows said to Parker.

"What about the accountant?" said Orwell.

"Don't count him out, Eddy."

Orwell waited until Willows and Parker had left the squad-room, and then turned to Spears and said, "Are we supposed to hold the guy, or what?"

"Maybe we should tell him his number's up," said Spears, and sneezed several times in quick succession.

Or was he laughing?

"What's so funny?" said Orwell, his face bunched up like a fist.

"Everything," said Spears, and wondered if he was going into remission.

19

The main branch of the city's public library is on the corner of Robson and Burrard, right downtown. The building is five storeys high — pre-formed concrete and big sheets of green-tinted glass.

Paterson knew what he wanted, but had no idea how to get it. He strolled by an unarmed guard in a natty gray uniform, made it past the library's swing-gate security system and walked up to a counter that had a sign hanging above it that said INFORMATION.

A plump woman with frizzy blonde hair listened carefully as he explained what he wanted, then directed him to the Sociology department. The librarian at Sociology was tall and thin, in his mid-thirties. He was wearing glasses with gold wire frames, a lemon-yellow shirt, neatly pressed brown pants, a brown tie decorated with gold horses.

"Excuse me," said Paterson. "Do you keep a clipping file on narcotics?"

The librarian nodded. A strand of mouse-brown hair fell across his forehead. He didn't seem to notice.

"Do you have anything on heroin?"

"Yes, we do. I'll need your library card, or two pieces of identification."

Paterson didn't own a library card, but he had a driver's licence, Visa.

The man disappeared behind a row of gray metal filing cabinets. A few moments later he reappeared carrying a buff-colored nine by twelve folder. He accepted Paterson's licence but ignored the credit card. The file was marked in bold typeface:

FOR REFERENCE SOCIOLOGY DIVISION VPL

NOT TO BE TAKEN FROM THIS ROOM

"Do you have any related files?"

The librarian nodded. "We have clippings on Crime, Narcotics, Youth and Drugs . . ." He adjusted the knot of his tie. The gold horses winced. "Would you like to see the file containing the subject headings?"

"Maybe later. Thanks for your help."

He took the folder over to a nearby table and sat down. The flap of the folder had been glued shut and then the folder had been sliced open along its length. He opened it and shook out a double handful of clippings.

The clippings varied in size from half a page or more to less than a hundred words. The smallest of them were glued to quarter-sheets of used computer paper. Each article was stamped in red ink with the name of the source newspaper and publication date. He noticed that they were all current. Presumably another file was kept for backdated clippings. If he needed to, he'd ask the librarian, see if he could squeeze a few more words out of him.

He pulled his chair a little closer to the table and went to work. A little over an hour passed before he found what he was looking for, a file from the *Vancouver Sun* in which a man named Gary Silk was found not guilty in County Court of possession with intent to traffic.

The drug was heroin, and the amount was large — a little over two kilos. It was the second time Silk had gone to trial, the second time he'd been acquitted.

There was a picture of Silk on the courthouse steps, flanked by his team of lawyers. He was smiling into the lens and looked like he was about fifteen years old, capable of anything. Near the end of the article it was noted that he lived in the city's Point Grey area, in a million-dollar house on Drummond Drive.

Paterson read through the rest of the clippings. There were half a dozen more articles on Gary Silk, all of them predating the trial. Paterson wrote down Silk's name and the name of the street he lived on. Then, on the spur of the moment, slipped the clipping file with Silk's picture into his shirt pocket.

He returned the folder to the desk, retrieved his driver's licence and went outside to the rank of public telephones. There was no listing for Gary Silk in the telephone book, not on Drummond

Drive or anywhere else in the city. He dropped a quarter and tried information. No luck. He went back to the information counter and, in general terms, told the blonde-haired woman what his problem was. She directed him to the City Directory, a thick volume which contained all the addresses in the city, the streets listed numerically or alphabetically, East side and West.

Paterson looked up Drummond Drive. There was no listing for Gary Silk but there were nine addresses on the street that had been listed either as 'vacant' or 'no return'.

Paterson wrote them down, double-checking to make sure he got it right.

Now what?

He went outside, turned to face the bustle of Robson, fondly called Robsonstrasse by the locals, because at one time the ethnic mix had been predominantly German. The street was still colorful and charming, the city's most pleasant walk. But the developers were moving in, rents were doubled and tripled as leases expired, new buildings catered to more affluent tenants. Shops that had once specialized in Bavarian sausages smoked on the premises now sold overpriced, mass-produced Italian leather goods. The street was in decline.

Paterson watched the swirl of the lunch-hour crowds along the sidewalks. He'd never felt like an outsider, but he felt like an outsider now.

There was a portable hot dog stand behind him, a white-painted plywood box with two oversized wheels, protruding wooden handles. The thing looked like a pregnant rickshaw. He ordered a hot dog with everything, a cup of coffee.

"Cream and sugar?"

"Just cream."

"That'll be two dollars and twenty-five cents." He gave the kid a five, stuffed the change in his pocket without counting it. He bit into the hot dog, sipped at his coffee. He was licking the last of the mustard from his fingers when it came to him.

Death and taxes.

You couldn't own property in the city without paying for the privilege.

Next stop, City Hall.

Paterson's footsteps echoed on the terrazzo floor of the central foyer. There was a circular information desk in the middle of the foyer. He had arrived during the lunch hour, and the desk was deserted. A cardboard sign next to a white push-button telephone said:

FOR INFO PLSE ENQUIRE CITY
CLERK'S OFFICE 3RD FLOOR OR PHONE 7276.

Paterson picked up the phone and dialled the four-digit number, explained his problem to a woman who directed him to the Tax Department. He asked for directions and she asked him which way he was facing, then told him to turn around.

"See the sign?"

"Yeah, thanks."

The line went dead. He cradled the phone. The Tax Department's sign hung over double glass doors on the far side of the foyer, directly in front of him and no more than thirty feet away.

The department was housed in a large, open room. Paterson lingered in the doorway, getting his bearings. There was a color-coded 'police yardstick' taped to the door frame. He entered the room, walked towards a woman standing behind the nearest of the two cashiers' wickets. The woman's head was bowed over a thick sheaf of pink paper. She glanced up as he drew near, smiled and said, "Can I help you?"

Paterson told her in general terms what he needed to know. There was a slim gold pencil tucked above the woman's ear, nestled in her hair. She removed the pencil and used it to point diagonally across the room. "See the woman in the white dress?"

Paterson nodded.

"That's Mrs Norquist. She'll be able to help you."

"Thank you."

Mrs Norquist was wearing oversized designer glasses with purple-tinted lenses, green plastic earrings shaped like miniature boomerangs. Apparently his situation wasn't all that unusual. She walked him over to a table in the middle of the open area. There were two large blue books on the table. One book contained all street addresses in the city; the second held the addresses of all the city's avenues.

"Instructions are on the inside cover."

Paterson pulled back a chair. "I'm looking for Drummond Drive. Would that be a street or an avenue?"

"Just follow the directions on the inside cover, you can't go wrong." She gave him an encouraging smile and walked away, glasses flashing under the lights, earrings in a holding pattern.

Paterson found Drummond Drive in the street index. There were thirty-six seven-digit account numbers on the street, each number representing a single address.

Each address also had an eleven-digit coordinate number.

Paterson checked his list of nine addresses taken from the City Directory, cross-referenced them against the addresses listed in the blue book. When he had coordinate numbers for all nine addresses he went over to the microfiche machines and sat down. The blue plastic slips of microfiche were arranged according to coordinate number, low to high. Paterson's lowest number was 101 635 018 16. The highest number was 109 635 030 63. All the numbers were on a single piece of microfiche. He looked up the addresses one by one, in the order that he'd happened to write them down.

The first property belonged to a man named Jason Williams and was valued for purposes of tax assessment at one million, forty thousand dollars. It seemed Gary Silk lived in a fairly decent neighborhood. Paterson moved to the next number. 4644 Drummond Drive was owned by a woman named Henrietta Porter, and her property was assessed at a little over half a million. He grinned. Maybe it wasn't such an expensive neighborhood after all.

He wrote Henrietta Porter's name next to her address, then moved on to the third eleven-digit account number.

When he'd finished, he had eight names, none of them Silk.

The ninth and last property, 1715 Drummond Drive, was owned by a registered company called Moody Investment Corporation, of 4411–1900 West Hastings. The notation BULK MAIL was on the microfiche above the corporation's address.

Paterson tracked down Mrs Norquist, who explained that the

notation BULK MAIL indicated that the company paid taxes on five or more properties in the city, and that all tax notices for those properties would be routinely mailed to the address on Hastings Street. He returned to the microfiche machine, switched off the light.

When he was a kid, his parents used to take him over to Vancouver Island for a couple of weeks every summer, to his Aunt Nell's beachfront cottage up the coast from Parksville. Low tide, they'd take short-handled shovels out to the flats and dig for clams. Aunt Nell used to say that when you'd finished shaking all the sand out of your bucket, what you had left was dinner.

Process of elimination.

Gary Silk lived on Drummond Drive but there was no listing for a Gary Silk on Drummond Drive. So it figured that Moody Investment Corporation had to be an alias for Gary Silk.

In a cul-de-sac off the foyer there were two cubicles containing public telephones. Paterson stepped into one and shut the door behind him. He flipped open the directory.

There was no listing for Moody Investment.

He tried the Yellow Pages, searched under 'Financial Planning Consultants', 'Investment Advisory Services', 'Dealers' and 'Financing'.

He tried 'Investment Management' and 'Investments Miscellaneous'.

No luck.

He dropped a quarter, dialled 411, gave the operator the company's full name and address and asked her if she had a recent listing. Zilch. The information came as no surprise, because by now he was convinced that Moody was a dummy company, no more substantial than a letterhead on a piece of paper. The Hastings Street address would turn out to be a lawyer's office. A dead end. Unless you had your own company, and happened to know how the game was played.

He went back to the Tax Department offices, sought out Mrs Norquist, told her she'd been very helpful and asked if he might have her card for future reference. A public employee, she was happy to oblige. The card was white, with plain black printing:

P. NORQUIST

TAX DEPARTMENT, CITY OF VANCOUVER

P. Norquist. Beautiful.

He thanked her once again for her help, slipped the card carefully into his wallet.

Outside, the air was still and warm and there was a light cloud cover over the city, a pale gray dusting of cirrus.

He hurried down the broad granite steps towards his Porsche. As he unlocked the car, it was twelve forty-seven by the big orange clock above City Hall. He drove downtown and made a brief stop at a store that specialized in office supplies, used his Visa card to buy a black spiral-bound notebook and a cheap leather briefcase with a built-in combination lock. At five minutes past two he pushed open a scuffed mahogany veneer door and entered the law offices of Morgan, Koestler and Brooks, located opposite the elevators on the fourth floor, 1900 West Hastings.

The office was a lot smaller than the big mahogany door suggested. There was a reception area containing a secretary's desk but no secretary, two leather chairs for waiting clients, a coffee table and a stack of outdated magazines, an ashtray that needed cleaning. There was a neat stack of business cards on the desk beside the typewriter. The cards were a glossy white, with plain black text. Acting on impulse, Paterson picked up several of the cards and put them in his shirt pocket.

Beyond the receptionist's desk there was a single doorway. Paterson ran his hand across the typewriter's keyboard. Dust turned to mud. He realized he was sweating.

"Can I help you?"

Paterson jumped.

"You Morgan, Koestler or Brooks?"

"I'm Anthony Morgan."

Paterson flipped open his brand-new notebook. "I'd like to see the Minute Book for a company called Moody Investment Corporation."

"Excuse me?" The lawyer was short, about five foot six, and very thin. He was wearing tinted glasses and a dark blue three-piece suit over a pale blue shirt. His hair was blond, short, tightly curled. His tie was in a paisley pattern, green and purple silk.

Paterson jammed his sweaty hands in his pockets. "My name's Norquist. I'm with tax collections, City Hall." He handed the lawyer the card Mrs Norquist had given him.

"If there's a problem, Mr Norquist, I'd really prefer you phoned and made an appointment . . ."

Paterson ran his thumb over the IBM's keyboard, letting Morgan see the accumulated dust. "We've already made a number of calls to this office. Your answering machine's monologue soon wears thin. And yes, there *is* a problem. The property known as 1715 Drummond Drive, registered owner Moody Investment Corporation, is presently being used as a multiple family dwelling. A flagrant violation of the city's zoning laws, as I'm sure you're aware."

Morgan used a corner of Norquist's card to clean the gap between his front teeth. He said, "Have you talked to anyone up at the house?"

"We haven't even been able to gain access to the grounds."

The lawyer thoughtfully tapped the edge of the card on the desk. He had two problems. The Companies Act gave Norquist or any other citizen the right to examine the corporation's Minute Book. He might be able to stall Norquist for a day or two, but that was about as far as he could go without risking a formal complaint, which could result in his being called before the bar.

A second consideration was his desire to spare his client as much grief as possible. Which meant, despite his instincts to the contrary, gracefully cooperating with bureaucrats like Norquist.

"My secretary's gone for the rest of the day. An illness in the family. I'm afraid it's going to take me a few minutes to locate the file. In the meantime, why don't you make yourself comfortable?"

Paterson glanced at his watch. He scowled, sat down stiffly in one of the upholstered chairs and picked up a year-old copy of *People* magazine.

Morgan disappeared into the inner office, shutting the door behind him.

In his mind's eye, Paterson saw the lawyer walk over to his

desk, pick up his telephone and punch in the City Hall number on Norquist's card. He saw Norquist answer at her end, Morgan make sure he was speaking to the real Norquist and then hang up and sit there for maybe ten seconds, deciding whether or not to call the cops. He saw Morgan dial 911 . . .

The door opened. Morgan came into the room carrying a bound, thick blue folder. Paterson stood up and Morgan handed the folder to him.

Among other things, a Minute Book contains records of the company: memoranda of Incorporation; number and types of outstanding shares and share structures. It includes the company's Incorporation number, date of Incorporation and the company articles — the usually complex rules by which the company may be governed.

The Minute Book is also required by law to contain a register of members, officers and directors. The one hundred thousand shares of Moody Investment Corporation stock were all owned by a single individual — Gary Silk.

Paterson was closing the file when he noticed a telephone number scrawled on the inside cover. The first three digits were 224. Point Grey was one of the areas serviced by that exchange. He memorized the number, stood up, shut the book with a thump and tossed it on the coffee table, started towards the door. Anthony Morgan had been leaning against his absent secretary's desk, legs crossed as he casually lit a big Cuban cigar. He gave Paterson a startled look, managed to hide his confusion by puffing out his cheeks and vigorously extinguishing the match. "That's it? You're finished?"

"That'll do until next time," said Paterson.

"Get what you wanted?"

"Just about. Can you give me Mr Silk's home phone number?"

The lawyer hesitated. "I'm not at all sure he's in town. Why don't I have him give you a call . . ." He fumbled in the breast pocket of his dark blue suit for Norquist's card. "You can be reached at this number?"

"Not really," said Paterson, and reached out and snatched the card away.

20

The address Mel Dutton had given Willows was 3207 Brock, which turned out to be a small bottle-glass stucco bungalow with wood trim that needed painting, a roof that had been patched with several different colors of duroid shingles.

The front lawn was mostly moss, the sidewalk leading up to the house cracked and uneven.

Willows pulled back the screen door. Parker made a fist, knocked three times.

The woman who answered the door was in her late sixties or early seventies. She was wearing green slacks and a white blouse, fluffy pink mules. Her silvery hair was swept back in a bun. Her eyes were bright blue, lively and intelligent. She was wearing lipstick, but no makeup. "If this is a religious matter, I'm afraid I'm really not interested."

Parker wondered if she was Oscar Peel's mother. She showed the woman her badge.

"Police?" The woman put a hand to her heart and involuntarily took a step backwards, into the safety of her home.

"We'd like to talk to Mrs Peel," said Parker.

"Why, what's this all about?"

Parker glanced at Willows. "A personal matter," she said.

The woman nodded, relief flooding her face. "That poor child. It's about her husband, isn't it? She told me he'd run off."

"Is she home?" said Willows.

"I believe so."

"We'd like to talk to her, if you don't mind."

"Just follow the pathway around to the back. You'll see the door. If she doesn't answer, keep knocking. She likes to watch the soaps, and the TV's in her bedroom." She smiled at Parker.

"You gave me a terrible fright. Mayor Campbell and city council have been cracking down on basement suites, and it's such a worry. Property taxes are so high, and all I've got is my pension. If I didn't have the rent from downstairs, I'd lose my house."

Willows let go of the screen door and started down the steps.

"I don't know what harm it's doing. My husband built those rooms. They're warm and clean, and I don't charge very much. Not like what an apartment would cost. Mrs Peel has no idea where she and the baby would go if she had to leave . . ." She frowned. "You aren't going to tell them about me, are you?"

"Absolutely not," said Parker. "We won't say a word, I promise you."

The door to the basement suite had been painted an aggressively cheerful yellow. There was a door knocker in the shape of a woodpecker. The bird had a glossy red body and red tail feathers, a sharp black beak and eyes the same shade of blue as the landlady's. Jack Willows was reminded of a distant mountain glade, a white corpse gliding silently through black water. Inside, they could hear the blare of a television.

"*The Dating Game*," said Parker. "Ever watch it?"

"Not yet."

"It's fascinating," said Parker. "You wonder, what are these people doing? Did they play a variation of the same game back in the Middle Ages, during the plague?" She reached out and gripped the woodpecker's tail, used it to lever the beak into a varnished stump that had been cut from a short length of alder. The beak hitting the stump made a sound about as loud as a pencil tapped on the surface of a distant desk. The bird, it seemed, was more decorative than functional.

"Bachelor number two," blared the television.

Willows made a fist, thumped his knuckles repeatedly against the wood.

Inside the apartment, a telephone began to ring. A moment later the television abruptly died.

"Now," said Parker.

Willows pounded on the door. No response. The door was locked. He stepped back and kicked it, leaving black scuff marks on the yellow paint.

"Who is it?"

"Police," said Willows.

"Beat it!"

"It's about Oscar," said Parker. Willows admired the effortless way she was able to raise her voice without seeming to shout.

They heard the thud of a withdrawn deadbolt. The door swung open three inches and was stopped by a chain thick enough to anchor a freighter.

"Lemme see your shields."

Willows opened his wallet; Parker dug in her purse. They held up their gold detective's shields and the chain rattled and the door swung wide.

"C'mon in. The place is a mess, but that's the way I like it."

The ceiling was low, about seven feet high. Heating ducts from the furnace further reduced the height between the living-room and kitchen. Closed doors led to what Willows guessed was the bedroom and bathroom. It was hot in the apartment, the air dry and stuffy. He could still hear the television. The phone was off the hook. There were dirty pots on the stove and the smell of burnt meat permeated the air.

"So what's the problem?" Oscar Peel's wife was a bleached blonde. Her hair was cut short at the sides and long at the back, combed into a froth over her forehead. She was about five feet tall and weighed maybe a hundred pounds. She was wearing a bulky burgundy cardigan and faded jeans cinched tight around her narrow waist with a silver-buckled cowboy belt, knee-length black leather boots. Willows guessed her age at eighteen or nineteen.

Parker pointed at the telephone dangling at the end of its cord. "Did you want to take care of that?"

"Oh yeah, sure." Mrs Peel picked up the phone. "I got somebody here, they just dropped in. Call you back in a few minutes." She hung up as she finished speaking, without waiting for a response.

"It's about your husband," said Parker. "Would you like to sit down for a minute?"

"Oscar's dead, is that it?"

Parker nodded. The widow Peel stared at her for a moment and then glanced towards Willows, as if seeking a second opinion, confirmation. A vent gushed hot air into Willows' face. He blinked, moved to one side, took off his jacket.

"We'd like you to come down to the morgue with us and identify him," said Willows. He added, "But it's Oscar, no question."

Behind the door that Willows had guessed led to the bedroom, there was a dull thud and then the sudden wail of a baby.

"Oh, Christ. Just wait a minute, will you."

The widow Peel pushed the door open and went into the bedroom and slammed the door shut behind her. The crying doubled in intensity and volume. The door opened and she came out carrying a baby wrapped in a pale blue blanket. She sat on a sagging tartan sofa, lifted her sweater and gave the infant her breast, lit a cigarette, scratched at a sticky brown substance that had spilled across the arm of the sofa. "You gonna tell me what happened to him, or do I have to guess?"

"He was shot through the back of the head," said Willows. "Somebody executed him. We thought you might be able to help us find out who did it."

"I got no idea, believe me. Oscar was the kind of guy everybody liked, real easy to get along with." She blew a stream of smoke at the ceiling. "I doubt if he had any enemies, tell you the truth. If he was shot, it was probably a case of mistaken identity."

"You think so, huh?"

"I wouldn't be at all surprised, really."

Parker sat down on the sofa. Mother and child ignored her. "She's a lovely baby," said Parker. "What's her name?"

"Rebecca."

The baby was switched from the left breast to the right. Willows had been caught looking. The grieving widow gave him a winsome smile.

"Since your husband was shot four times at close range," said Parker, "I seriously doubt it was a mistake." She raised her voice, and this time it did seem as if she was shouting, even though she wasn't. "Are you listening to me, young lady!"

The ash on Tracy Peel's cigarette was an inch long. It fell to the carpet.

"If you know of any trouble that Oscar was in, a drug deal, somebody he . . ."

"Oscar wasn't involved in drugs."

"Somebody he owed money . . . Another woman."

"And he was a good husband. Hardly ever went out, was happy to stay home and be with the baby."

"Then why won't you help us?" Parker said.

"Because I'm scared what happened to Oscar could happen to me."

"Did somebody threaten you?"

"Walt threatened me."

Parker sat down on the sofa. She risked putting an arm around the girl's shoulders. She could smell hair spray, perfume, deodorant, nail polish, stale beer. She said, "Who's Walt?"

"My case worker. He's with MHR. Warned me he had his eye on me. Said all I had to do was make one little mistake and he'd seize Rebecca."

Willows glanced around the tiny apartment, at the dirt and grime, unwashed dishes, overflowing ashtrays, the plastic bags of garbage stacked against the wall by the door. MHR was the Ministry of Human Resources. He sniffed the air, wondered where the diaper basket was and how long it'd been since the widow Peel had been to the laundromat.

"If you think of anything . . ." said Parker. She gave Tracy Peel her card.

The door wasn't quite slammed shut. The deadbolt thudded home, they heard the rattle of the chain. Parker started up the short flight of concrete steps to ground level, but Willows loitered, waiting for the blare of the television. ". . . bachelor number one, it says here that you're an aspiring actor, and that you'd like to get involved in the production end of . . ."

The baby started crying again.

"What d'you think?" said Parker when they were back in the car.

"Notice how hot it was in there?"

"Yeah, I noticed."

"She was wearing a sweater. The sleeves rolled down. You heard the baby crying. Saw the way she handled her cigarette . . ."

"You think she was wired?"

"That's what it looked like to me."

"Up there," said Parker, "and not quite ready to come down."

"Prime time junkie heaven."

Parker rolled down her window. "Oscar was a dealer."

"That's right, he was." Willows started the car and fastened his seatbelt.

"Is that why you didn't push her to come down to the morgue, because she was high?"

"No rush," Willows said. "They can fine-tune him after the autopsy, make him a little more presentable."

"You think she already knew about him, that he'd been killed?"

"Wouldn't surprise me, the way she reacted."

Parker had a sudden, horrifying thought. "What about the baby, Rebecca?"

"If Tracy's an addict, and she's breast feeding her, then the kid's an addict too."

"A baby junkie."

"I wonder who's dealing to her mother," Parker said.

"Maybe Walt can tell us."

"Just what I was thinking."

"Sure you were," said Willows. He grinned. "But I said it first."

Pat Nash waited until he heard the door slam shut, counted to ten and then cranked the TV back up. Hard to believe the way the three guys sitting up there on the stools were making fools of themselves. The broad didn't sound too bad, had a nice sexy voice. But if they could see what she looked like, they'd trample all over each other trying to get out of the studio.

Or maybe not. Maybe they were the kind of guys who were willing to eat cold leftover shit to get on TV, a shot at a free trip to Burbank, wherever the hell that was.

Tracy came into the room. Pat smiled at her. She looked so cute, holding the babe. It really turned him on, motherhood.

"What'd they say?" he asked her.

"Wanted to know who killed Oscar. Wanted me to solve the fucking case for them."

"What'd you tell 'em?"

"Nothing, not a fuckin' word."

Nash stretched out on the bed. "She's gonna pick bachelor number one," he said, "and believe me, the guy is the world's biggest dink."

"Maybe that's what she's after."

"Hey," Nash said, "don't talk dirty."

The baby had gone to sleep. Tracy put her in the crib, pulled the little blanket over her body. "Think they know anything?"

"What day it is, maybe."

"There were two of them, detectives. A man and a woman."

"Yeah?"

"The woman was real pretty. She was wearing a dark blue suit, and she had jet black hair, glossy and clean looking, like a raven's wing."

"I've always kind of liked blondes," said Pat Nash. He patted the bed. "Get your ass over here."

"The way you sweet talk me, it's irresistible."

Nash struggled to a sitting position. He drew up his knees and pushed himself backward, leaned against the wall. "We're both nervous. A couple more days, it'll be over."

"How much money did that guy Frank say we're gonna get? What'd he say our share was gonna be?"

"Twenty percent of a million. Two hundred grand."

"Can you trust him?"

"More than he can trust me."

Tracy looked down at the sleeping baby. "It's a lot of money."

"Not enough, baby."

"What d'you mean?"

Nash reached out and grabbed her by the arm and pulled her on to the bed. He reached into the pocket of her ratty burgundy cardigan for her cigarettes, lit up.

"Frank wants me to do Gary. I figure, why the hell not do both of them, while I'm at it? Take all the money. The whole million. Frank did Oscar, right? Shot him in cold blood."

Tracy Peel leaned in on Nash and rested her hand, fingers splayed, on his chest.

Nash said, "Pow! Pow! Sweet dreams, Frankie."

"Gimme a kiss," said Tracy. She could feel Nash's chest hair, crinkly and stiff, beneath the thin cotton of his shirt. Oscar had been almost hairless. Even on his legs and under his armpits, there was hardly enough to notice. It was the one and only thing she hadn't liked about him.

Her mouth on Pat Nash's, she wondered when the cops would come back, drag her off to the morgue to make her look at whatever was left of the only man she'd ever loved.

21

The telephone burbled, a soft, disinterested, happy sound—like a baby full of warm milk.

Gary kept watching the game.

Lazy bastard.

Frank pushed himself up off the rug and ambled over to the bar. He picked up the phone and said, "Yeah, who is it?" He held the phone pressed up against his ear, frowned but didn't say anything.

Frank and Gary and the juicer were watching a ball game on TV, the New York Yankees and Oakland Athletics. Somebody scored, an Athletic, but Gary didn't notice who it was because his eyes had glazed over. Bottom of the seventh inning and Billy Martin, who was the Yankees' manager at the time, still hadn't kicked dirt on any of the umpires. Christ, what was the game coming to.

The TV broke to a commercial. A blonde girl wearing a slinky black evening dress and diamond earrings tried to sell them a Ford. Or maybe it was a Chevrolet. Frank still hadn't said a goddamn word. Gary drank some beer. Snapped his fingers and lifted his eyebrows, gave Frank a look that said — Hey, what's up?

Frank paid no attention to Gary, he *still* hadn't said anything. He was nodding his head as if the guy on the other end could see him and it was important that he seem to be cooperating.

"Who the fuck is it, Frank?" Gary's patience, what there was of it, had been exhausted in the space of about thirty seconds.

Frank cupped his hand over the receiver. "Guy says he found something valuable that he figures you must've lost. Won't say what it is. Says he found it last weekend, washed up on the beach in a plastic bag. Wants to know if there's a reward."

Gary poked Samantha in the ribs. She gave him a look and he gave her that same look right back and said, "Take a hike, sweetie."

"Where to, Gary?"

"Try the kitchen."

"What'm I supposed to do in the kitchen?"

"Clean the oven, baby." Gary gave her a nice smile. "With your tongue."

"Okay, okay. I'm leaving." Samantha stood up. "You don't have to be such a grouch, that's all."

"Hey, you ain't seen nothin' yet." Gary rolled up his subscription copy of *Time* and whacked her on the ass, like she was a puppy that had made the mistake of baring its puppy teeth. He watched her skitter across the room and out the door. Sad to say, but it was getting to the point where the girl had just about worn out her welcome.

Frank hung up. He glanced at Gary, shrugged.

"Lemme guess," Gary said. "Marcel Marceau?"

"Huh?" said Frank.

"What I'm asking, who the hell was it?"

"He didn't give me a name, Gary. Just said what I already told you, we lost something and he's got it. And how much is it worth to us to get it back."

"You recognize the voice? Was it that sneaky little punk Randy DesMoines?"

"I don't know who it was. Not Randall, though. Guy said he wants to set up a meet."

"That'd be nice."

"The Varsity Grill, of all places."

"What, that place over on Tenth Avenue, we get the takeout Chinese, Special Won-Ton?"

Frank looked at his watch. "You're supposed to be there in ten minutes."

"Okay, let's go."

"Just you, Gary."

Gary Silk chewed his lower lip. "What's the nearest cross street?"

"Trimble."

"Okay, I'll drop you at Trimble a couple blocks below Tenth. You can trot the rest of the way, it'll take you maybe two or three minutes. When you get there, sit down as close to us as possible."

"What if there's no empty booths? That's a popular restaurant, Gary."

"Then stand and wait, okay? Just like you're an ordinary customer."

"I don't like Chinese food, you know that."

"Jesus Christ!" yelled Gary.

"Just kidding," said Frank, wounded.

In the garage, Frank got even with Gary by pretending he couldn't find the keys to the Caddy. Gary made nasty metallic clicking sounds with his tongue. Frank put a stop to that by dropping his .44 calibre Magnum Research Desert Eagle on Gary's foot. The gun looked big enough to shoot dinosaurs, and the weight of it sent Gary hopping and shrieking across the oil-stained cement like a demented little gap-toothed one-legged bunny.

"You big dope!" screamed Gary.

"Sorry," said Frank.

Frank pulled the Caddy over at Eighth and Trimble, across the street from the park. There was a church on the corner, but if God was home he didn't have any lights on. Frank opened the car door and slid out from behind the wheel, stepped on to the street.

"Wanna borrow my gun, Gary?"

Gary said, "Hey, what kind of guy you think I am? The service is *that* bad, I'll eat someplace else." He slammed the door shut and took off, the Caddy rocketing through the intersection.

"Is that a no?" said Frank. He started walking. The Caddy's brake lights flared as Gary turned left on Tenth Avenue.

When Frank walked into the restaurant, he saw Gary right away. Or rather, he saw the back of Gary's head, the mousse or gel or whatever it was he used making his hair look slick and kind of slimy under the lights. Gary was in a two-seater near the back of the restaurant, down by the soft-drink cooler. All the other booths in the place were occupied. Frank sat down at the counter. A waiter ambled past and he ordered a cup of coffee and a donut.

"No donuts. All gone! You like a cookie, great big cookie?"

"Just coffee," said Frank. He'd seen the waiter somewhere before, not in the restaurant. He recognized him, but couldn't place him. Was the guy a cop? The way he carried himself, Frank didn't think so.

He was about ten feet away from Gary's booth. Gary was digging into a bowl of Special Won-Ton. Using a fork. The restaurant was noisy, and Frank couldn't quite make out what was being said. Gary's dinner companion, obviously the guy who made the phone call, seemed to be doing most of the talking.

Frank slurped his coffee and turned casually towards them. The guy sitting opposite Gary was in his late forties, dressed in a tan sports jacket, slacks. He could've been a cop, businessman, low-life drug dealer. Helicopter pilot. Off-duty priest. Christ, anything. He looked up and caught Frank's eye. Frank turned his attention to the television suspended above the last booth along the far wall. Bottom of the ninth and it was the Yankees over Oakland, seven to six. Frank glanced back at the guy in the suit. The guy was staring at him. Frank got busy with his coffee. There'd been something in the guy's eyes — he knew what Frank was up to and plainly didn't give a shit. Had it all figured out, it seemed.

"You like the coffee?" It was the waiter. Frank remembered where he'd seen him. Or at least someone who looked like him — the guy who played Jack Lord's buddy on that old TV series, *Hawaii Five-O*.

"Coffee's fine," Frank said.

"Want more cream?"

"No, it's okay."

"You don't like the coffee, I don't charge you. Not one penny. Okay?"

"Okay," said Frank.

The waiter bunched up his eyebrows and glanced over Frank's shoulder. Frank spun around on his stool to look behind him. Gary was moving towards him, brushing past the soft-drink machine, his hands in his pockets and a toothpick in his mouth. Frank craned his neck to check out the booth. It was empty.

"Where the fuck is he?" Frank said.

Gary said, "Don't worry about it, your face'll go all wrinkly." He handed Frank a brown paper bag that weighed about half a pound.

"What's this?"

"Possession with intent. For a first offense, about five years in the slammer."

"Or half a pound of baking soda."

"Maybe," said Gary, "but I don't think so. I mean, what would be the point?"

Frank dropped a dollar on the counter. They started towards the door.

"We should've bagged him," said Frank. "Gone to bed happy."

"Or got shot in the knee like Randall DesMoines." Gary waited for Frank to open the door for him, stepped out on to the sidewalk.

"He had a gun?"

"An automatic. A twenty-two. Gave me a little poke in the belly when I sat down. Kept it pointed at me the whole time we talked."

"He got the twenty kilos?"

"Found it washed up on the beach in West Van. Wants five hundred grand. He's coming to the house tomorrow night, to do the exchange."

Frank's broad face registered disbelief. "He agreed to come to us?"

"You betcha."

"All by himself? And trust you to be a sweet guy and hand over the cash?"

"He's got a friend," said Gary. "Also, a tape of the little talk we just had in the restaurant. We try to screw him, he isn't out of the house two minutes after he walks inside, his pal phones the cops. Tells them what went down. Gives them the tape." Gary shrugged. It was about as philosophical as he ever got. "He's a fuckin' businessman, Frank. His price is too low to haggle over, and he knows it. Anyhow, I figure the town's so dry I can jack up my price, absorb the loss."

"Good thinking," said Frank. "So you're actually gonna do the deal?"

"I've dropped half a mil in a weekend at Vegas," Gary said. "The guy's being reasonable. Just this once, I'm gonna do things the easy way."

"Half a mil," said Frank. His shoulders slumped. He'd figured at least twice that much. On the other hand, looking on the bright side, a low number was all the more reason not to do a split with Nash.

"What would you've done?" said Gary.

"Told him five hundred grand wasn't even close, he should've asked for a whole lot more."

Gary laughed and slapped Frank on the back so hard it made him break stride. They walked down Tenth Avenue to the car. Frank made a U-turn and took them home, to the house on Drummond Drive.

They found Samantha in the kitchen, standing at the counter dropping Florida oranges into an automatic press, pouring the juice into a highball glass full of chunk ice, mixing Tom Collinses just about as fast as she could knock them down.

"Make it three," said Gary. He bent over her and brushed her hair back and bit her on the neck hard enough to bring tears to her eyes.

"Hey, what'd I do to you?"

"Everything either one of us could think of," said Gary. He slid his hand down the front of her sweater, winked at Frank. Frank looked away. Samantha kept dropping oranges into the machine. Gary held on for a few seconds, long enough to make his point, and then withdrew his hand from her sweater and wandered over to the fridge. "I hardly touched my Won-Ton. Should've got 'em to wrap it for me. Put it in one of them wax boxes with the wire handles. Want something to eat, Frank? A burger, maybe? With bacon and cheese, fried onions?"

"It's too late at night, it'll make me dream."

"So?"

"Give me indigestion, Gary."

"Bullshit." Gary tossed Frank a two-pound package of raw hamburger. "Get cooking, kiddo." He went over to Samantha and tousled her hair, making a mess of it. "Wanna burger, sweets?"

"No thanks, Gary."

Gary made a hissing sound, like air leaking out of a slow snake on a fast road. "Make it three, Frank."

Frank was crouched down in front of the oak kitchen cabinets to the right of the sink, scrambling around like a goddamn maid, trying to find a frying pan. He nodded but didn't say anything, not trusting his voice. And he kept his face averted so Gary couldn't see the look in his eyes.

Because if Gary saw what he was thinking, he'd head straight for the door. Frank didn't want to have to play tag. Gary was too fast, because of all those miles he jogged. Anyhow, the time wasn't right. Tomorrow night, Frank'd take care of Nash and whoever else happened to be around. Grab the heroin and money, and then hit Gary. Catch him flat-footed. Do him painful, but do him quick.

Yeah, painful but quick.

The three of them sat at the kitchen table and ate hamburgers and ripple chips and drank Samantha's vague idea of what a Tom Collins should taste like. The meat was overcooked and there was too much gin in the drinks, but what Gary kept going on about was Samantha's table manners.

"Hey, baby. Slow down. What is this, a table or a fuckin' trough? Frank."

"Yeah, Gary."

"She eats like a bird, wouldn't you say?"

Frank waited.

"A fuckin' pelican!" said Gary. His laugh was like someone slamming the lid down on a garbage can. There was chunky green hamburger gunk on his chin. He wiped his mouth on his shirtsleeve. "Know what the Heimlich maneuver is, Frank? Where somebody's choking on a big hunk of meat and you put your arms around them and give 'em a squeeze?"

Frank shook his head. The Tom Collinses were giving him a monster headache, a real skull cruncher. He got up and went to the fridge, grabbed a Coors.

Gary poked Samantha in the ribs, making her wince. "This the last meal of the summer? You stuff your face and then crawl under the table and hibernate till spring, that what happens?"

Gary winked at Frank but Frank pretended not to notice, concentrated on pouring his beer. He'd seen it all before. First Gary started pounding on them with words, and then, if they didn't take the hint, he went at them with his fists. The way Samantha was gnawing on her burger, Frank figured her for one of the smart ones.

When Gary had finally finished eating and drinking and burping and being critical, he got down to business.

"We're gonna need a junkie. Somebody who knows how to appreciate a good rush."

"Or a chemist," Frank said. "You think he messed around with the dope?"

"Why would he risk it? On the other hand, why should we take the chance? Give Randall a call and tell him to send somebody over."

"When?" said Frank.

"Tomorrow night." Gary was stroking Samantha's arm, his hand crooked like a big spider, his fingernails leaving pale streaks in her flesh. "Tell Randy I want him here at ten o'clock sharp."

"Maybe," said Frank slowly, "it'd be a good idea to have Pat Nash here, too."

"Why?"

Frank rubbed his chin. He said, "Nash owes you a big one. All those people around, maybe you could use him."

Gary thought about it. He said, "You worried about Randy, is that it?"

"And the businessman. We don't really know who he is, anything about him. You said he's got a gun. Maybe he plans to use it."

Gary leaned back in his chair. One of the Siamese cats wandered into the kitchen. It saw Gary and hurried out. "Okay," Gary said. "Give Nash a call, too."

"I'll go have a beer somewhere," said Frank. "Use a pay phone to call Randall."

Gary nodded. He had his nails deep into Samantha's arm, was getting himself all lathered up.

Frank stood up, patted himself down. He turned his pockets inside out, frowned his displeasure.

"What?" said Gary.

"The phone call," said Frank. "I ain't got any change. Can you lend me a quarter?"

Gary leaned over and grabbed Samantha's purse and zipped it open, rummaged around inside.

Frank drove Gary's Caddy down Tenth, turned right on Dunbar. At Dunbar and Thirtieth there was a neighborhood pub, a wine and cheese joint. Frank ordered a cold plate and pint of draft beer. He drank half the pint, studied the clock over the bar. Five past eleven. He glanced at his watch. Check. There was a pay phone by the door. He got Randall DesMoines' number out of his wallet and punched buttons. He couldn't tell if the phone was ringing or not because of the TV over the bar, plus an old couple in a corner singing mournfully in a language he'd never heard before, but was maybe Gaelic, because they were both wearing tams.

A voice, shrill as a tin whistle, sounded in his ear. He said, "Lemme speak to Randall."

"Who is it?"

"Tell him, Frank."

"Frank who?"

"Frank Lloyd Wright."

The girl giggled. "Mr Right, huh. I knew you'd come along sooner or later."

Frank went back to his table and drained his pint, signalled to his waitress for a refill. When he got back to the phone, Randall was waiting for him, whining apologies.

"Who was the bimbo?" Frank said.

"I dunno. Just somebody wandered in. A party girl, know what I mean?"

"No idea," said Frank. He could hear Michael Jackson in the background, the percussive thud of drums. Randall had a weird taste in music. "Turn that shit off," Frank said.

The music died instantly. Randall must've had a remote control.

"What's up, Randall?"

"Whatever."

"Gary wants some company."

"No shit," said Randall. "You mean a real woman, all growed up? Way I heard it, he likes to cruise the juice bars and ice-cream parlors. Skim the young stuff."

"This is business," said Frank. "Remember the guy in the hotel?"

"Whenever I take my doberman for a walk. I get ahold of him, Tyson's gonna have himself a real good time."

"Who?" said Frank.

"My dog. Tyson. I named him after the boxer."

"What boxer? Didn't you just say he was a doberman?"

"I said he . . ." Randall hesitated. "You pulling my leg?"

"And you can make book it's the only part of you I'll ever pull." When Frank finally stopped laughing he said, "We just spent some time with the guy who popped you. A natural-born salesman, real smooth. Gave us back some of our product. Gary wants to run a test, see if it's tasty as it looks."

"I know a chemist," said Randall. "Give him a couple twists, he'll take care of you."

"Bring a woman. Gary wants to watch her shoot up, see what happens."

"I don't much like that idea," said Randall. "That girl Moira's still fresh in my mind, know what I mean? Jeez, I'd hate to lose another one."

Frank waited. After about ten seconds, Randall caved in.

"What time you want her there?"

"Ten o'clock sharp."

"It's already past eleven!"

"Tomorrow night, Randall. That give you time to get organized, or should I tell Gary you can't make it?"

"We'll be there," Randall said.

Frank disconnected. He used another of the juicer's quarters to dial the number Pat Nash had given him. A woman answered. Frank asked for Nash. She asked him who was calling. He didn't say anything. The phone made a clunking sound. In the background, he could hear what sounded like a baby crying.

Nash came on the line. Frank told him where and when. He hung up and went back to his table. Still a nice head on his beer. He sipped. It was twenty past eleven. Gary'd be wondering where he was. Well, fuck Gary. The Caddy was a V-6 and had about as much acceleration as a wheelbarrow, but he could still make it back to Drummond Drive in under ten minutes, if he hit the lights. He got home a little late, he'd lie and say the line was busy, he had to call back.

He tilted his head back and emptied the pint, caught the waitress' eye. He was pretty thirsty, for a guy who did his best work when he was sober. He told himself all he was doing was trying to drown the godawful hamburger Gary had stuffed down his throat, but that wasn't it and he knew it.

Truth was, Gary was driving him to drink.

Truth was, Frank could hardly wait to blow the dumb bastard right off the face of the map.

22

Half a ring, and then the answering machine cut in.

"You there, Parker?" It was Sergeant Curtis, of the Marine Squad.

It was early, a few minutes past seven. Parker was in the kitchen, waiting with dwindling patience for the last of her breakfast coffee to dribble through the filter and into the pot. She stared at the answering machine, the slowly turning cassette.

There was a pause, and then Curtis said, "I've been trying to get in touch with Jack. He isn't answering his phone."

The toast popped. Parker reached for the butter.

"Reason I'm calling," said Curtis, "Removal Services just returned Oscar Peel's body bag. I don't know if you were aware of this, but they always clean the bags before they give them back to us."

Parker poured coffee into two mugs, added cream from a black and white container in the shape of a cow.

The machine continued to run as Curtis said, "I gave Leyton the job of stowing the bag back in the boat. He found something I think you'll find pretty interesting."

Parker waited, knife in hand, over the cooling and forgotten toast.

"Give us a call," said Curtis, and hung up.

What Leyton had found in the bottom of the body bag was a rectangle of polished metal about three inches wide by five inches long and approximately half an inch deep. In the middle of the rectangle were two jagged, rusting stumps. There was an engraved inscription:

3rd Place
Men's Singles
1988 Inter-City Squash Championships

"It's the base of some kind of trophy," Curtis said.

"You play squash?" said Willows.

"Not really."

"Know anybody who does?"

"Nope."

Willows looked at Constable Leyton, who grinned and said, "I feel the need for some exercise, I walk the dog around the fire hydrant down at the end of the block."

"Try the daily papers," said Parker. "The sports columnists."

Willows picked up the phone and started dialling. No one at either of the city's two major dailies would admit to any knowledge of the tournament. Both papers were owned by the same company and shared the same building. Willows asked if he could gain access to the library to research back issues. He was told it was possible, but he'd be required to pay a thirty-dollar per hour fee. It was also necessary to get clearance from the Head Librarian, who was on holiday and not expected back until the end of the following week.

Willows disconnected. He turned to Curtis. "Got a Yellow Pages?"

Curtis slid open a drawer, handed Willows the phone book.

Willows turned to Health Clubs. Walked his fingers down the page until he found a local club that had squash courts, dialled the number.

"Bodyworks, may I help you?" A woman's voice, thin and chirpy, professionally cheerful.

"This is Detective Jack Willows, Vancouver Police. I want to talk to your squash pro."

"Jay?"

There was a pause.

"I'd like to ask him a few questions, that's all. About a local tournament."

"Jay's from back east. Toronto. He moved here just a few months ago. I really don't think . . ."

"Tell him I'd like to talk to him, will you."

"He isn't in at the moment. As a matter of fact, he isn't due to start work until four o'clock."

"What's his home number?"

"One moment, please."

Willows heard the shuffling of paper. The telephone clattered on the desk.

He hung up, dialled the number of another downtown fitness club. The pro had been let go. Lack of demand. Willows explained his problem. He was given another number, and a name. He dialled and got a busy signal. Slammed the phone down.

"We had a direct line to everywhere," said Curtis, "just think of the time we'd save."

Willows tried the number again. The phone rang five times, was picked up by a kid with a lisp, who sounded about ten years old.

"UBC Squash Courts."

Willows identified himself. "I'd like to speak to Rich Woodward."

"He isn't here."

Christ. "Do you know where I can reach him?"

"He could be in the gym. Try the weight room. Or maybe the pool."

"Is there a phone?"

"What d'you mean?"

"Is there a phone number for the gym or pool?"

"Oh yeah, sure. Hang on a minute."

Willows was given two numbers. Rich Woodward hadn't used the weight room. He'd just left the pool.

"Do you know where I might be able to reach him?"

"Probably the squash courts. Want the number?"

A different kid answered when Willows called back. Willows identified himself and said he'd been told that Woodward was on his way over. Would the kid please tell him that Willows wanted to ask him a few questions and should be there within the hour?

"No problem. He's got two forty-five minute bookings. Reserved the court for an hour and a half, is what I mean. It's a regular thing with him, six days a week. He'll be playing until . . . lemme see . . . about half-past twelve. After that he'll . . ."

Willows hung up. Parker and Curtis stared idly out the window. Willows scooped up the evidence bag, stuffed it in his jacket pocket. He started for the door.

"Drop by some time," Curtis said to Parker. He smiled. "We're on duty until midnight, be glad to take you out for a tour. The harbor looks real nice by starlight."

"I'll keep it in mind," said Parker. Through the open doorway, she could see that Willows was already halfway to the car.

Willows drove through the downtown core and along Beach, past the stone Inuit sculpture that was no doubt authentic but to his way of thinking cluttered up the shoreline. They sped over the Burrard Street Bridge, along Point Grey Road and South West Marine Drive past the beaches and then up a winding road through a scrim of hardwoods to the sprawling campus of the University of British Columbia.

"Still know your way around?" said Parker.

"Not so much anymore." It had been almost twenty years since Willows had graduated. In the interim he'd taken a few criminology courses, but always at the city's other major university, Simon Fraser. He braked to let a clutch of blue-jeaned students cross the road, wondered if he'd ever looked that young, that aimless.

"Ever come out to Freddy Wood?" said Parker.

"The theatre?"

"Right."

"Haven't seen a play in years."

Willows made a sharp right and found himself driving the wrong way down a dead-end street. He made a hasty U-turn. At the intersection an RCMP cruiser drifted past — the campus and Endowment Lands were patrolled by the Royal Canadian Mounted Police.

"Why don't you ask him for directions?" said Parker, glancing over her shoulder at the cruiser.

"We're doing fine."

"You ever see that Mountie you met up in Squamish, Pat Rossiter?"

"He quit the force. Moved to town and went to work for a private detective agency."

"But you don't stay in touch?"

"He called a couple of times, trying to chase up some business. It's been a while since I've heard from him. Couple of months, at least."

They drove past the university bookstore. Willows remembered it as being much smaller, and in a different location. He came to another intersection, made a left turn on the yellow. A girl in a short black dress and cowboy boots stared at him. Her boyfriend said something and laughed. Willows glanced in his rearview mirror.

The RCMP cruiser was right behind them, headlights flashing.

Willows pulled over to the curb, got out of the car and walked swiftly back to the cruiser. The RCMP officer was in his early twenties. He glanced up, startled, as Willows reached the cruiser. The Mountie pushed open the car door and Willows stepped back, giving him room.

"Can you tell me how to get to the squash courts?" Willows said.

The Mountie flipped open his ticket book. "May I see your driver's licence, please."

"Sure," said Willows.

"Would you please take your licence out of . . ." The Mountie saw the gold detective's shield, leaned forward to take a closer look.

"The squash courts . . ." prompted Willows.

"There's a T-shaped intersection about a mile down the road, maybe a little more. The sports complex is off to the left. You'll see it." He removed his peaked cap, yanked open the cruiser's door and tossed the cap on the seat. "Next time you think about making a turn without signalling, do yourself a favor and take a look in your rearview mirror, okay?"

"Thanks for your help," said Willows.

There are four squash and two racquetball courts in the UBC complex. The kid with the lisp was back at the desk. He told Willows that Rich Woodward was in the end court, number six. Willows asked for directions.

The kid gave Parker a big, uncomplicated smile. He locked his cash register and led them down a narrow concrete hallway and up a flight of stairs, past a white-painted door. Willows found himself standing at the top of the spectator's gallery — several rows of wooden bench seats that were separated from the courts by strong netting. He said, "We wanted to talk to him, not watch him play."

"He doesn't like interruptions. Won't talk to you until his court time's over. Anyhow, there's no way to get at him. The door's locked from the inside."

"Which one is Woodward?"

"The guy with the wristbands."

The ball caromed off the end wall, hit the leftside wall and began to drop. Woodward attacked, delivered a backhand smash. The ball smacked against the end wall an inch above the foul line, rolled slowly across the polished wooden floor.

Willows crooked two fingers in his mouth and uttered a long, piercing whistle.

Woodward glanced up at him. Willows showed him his badge. Woodward used his racket to point at the big electric clock on the wall. He jammed his racket under his arm and made a fist with both hands and opened and closed both fists three times in rapid succession.

"He's got another thirty minutes on the court," the kid translated.

The netting was thick nylon cord. Willows supposed he could probably find a knife somewhere, or a pair of scissors . . .

Parker said, "The last thing we want is a hostile witness, Jack." She turned to their guide. "Is there a restaurant in the building?"

"I'll show you."

The sports complex housed a hockey rink as well as the squash courts. High above one end of the rink, separated from the ice by a wall of glass, was a spacious lounge with a fast-food restaurant and well-stocked bar, scatter of tables on a thin, beige carpet. A girl in jeans and a bulky sweatshirt brought them menus. Parker ordered a tossed salad and tea, Willows a cheeseburger and a beer.

The rink was occupied by twenty or thirty young children and their mothers. Several of the children were skating with the aid of folding metal chairs. Willows tried to recall his childhood. He remembered the first time he'd fallen; how hard and unyielding the ice had been, the sudden shock of pain that had been much worse than the accompanying humiliation.

"You skate?" said Parker.

"I was a player. When I was about ten years old. Peewee league."

"When did you decide you wanted to be a cop, instead of a highly-paid professional athlete?"

"About the same time my father decided he was tired of getting up at dawn to drive me to the rink."

Willows smiled. Parker thought he had a nice smile, for a cop. She watched a girl in white tights and pink mittens and a matching pink toque describe a figure-eight and then raise her arms high above her head and spin in a tight circle, glide gracefully across the ice.

The girl in jeans arrived with their food.

Willows bit into his hamburger. He drank some beer. The beer was cold. The beer was good. Eating was often a disappointment but drinking was always a pleasure. In future, he'd have to remember to drink more and eat less.

"What's so funny?" said Parker.

"Life. How's the salad?"

"I've had worse. It's just that I can't remember when."

Willows drank some more beer, listened with pleasure to the shrill cries of the children, scrape of skate blades on ice. He checked his watch. Woodward's time was up. He wondered, how was it that no matter where he was or what he was doing, just as he was beginning to enjoy himself, it was inevitably time to do something else?

Willows and Parker walked into the locker room and found Rich Woodward with a T-shirt bunched up in his hand and a towel draped around his neck. Woodward was muscular, sweaty. He had short brown hair, no sideburns. Intense, dark brown eyes. A warrior of the courts, a jock. He gave Parker a quick second look, and Willows watched the residual combativeness and intensity from the game slowly leak out of him. Willows decided it would be best if Parker asked the questions.

Parker introduced herself, got straight to the point.

"Who placed third in the Men's Singles competition of the 1988 Inter-City Squash Championships, Rich?"

"Are you serious?"

"Very serious. We're investigating a murder. We were told you might be able to help us."

Woodward used the towel to wipe sweat from his face, combed his hair with his fingers. "If you'd asked me who won . . ."

"Who won?" said Parker.

"Me," said Woodward, and grinned. "A pro from over on the island was second. Charlie Rankin. The guy who came in third . . ."

Parker had her notebook out, pen ready.

"His name was Gary something. Gary Silk. Feisty little bastard. Real nasty temper. Looks sort of like a scaled-down John McEnroe. Bad winner, terrible loser. I mean, I can be as intense as the next guy, but he was an asshole *all* the time, on and off the court."

"Gary Silk," said Parker. She spelled Silk's name as she wrote it down.

Woodward nodded. "That's it. What'd he do?"

"Can you describe him?" said Parker.

Woodward frowned. "I just did."

"Let me put it this way," said Parker. "Can you describe John McEnroe?"

Woodward snapped the sweatbands on his wrists to hide his confusion.

Willows said, "I think we've got what we came for, Claire." He shook Woodward's hand. "Thanks, Rich."

"Hey, any time."

Outside, walking across the parking lot towards the car, Parker said, "So now I know why you stopped playing hockey. You were afraid you'd turn into a dumb jock."

"No stereotyping," said Willows. "It's departmental policy, if I recall."

23

"Get your warrant, Jack?"

"An hour ago."

Inspector Bradley nodded. It had been a bright and sunny day. The natural light so strong he hadn't needed to turn on the goddamn overhead fluorescents that usually buzzed and hissed and crackled all day long, like a great big bowl of cereal, distracting him and with increasing frequency making it next to impossible to concentrate on his work.

Now it was past seven; the sky had begun to darken and the walls of his office were magically turning the color of cherry blossoms. He wriggled a little lower in his chair, puffed on his cigar.

His belly growled. He was very hungry, but somehow had no appetite. Recently his dining habits had changed dramatically. Cooking had suddenly become a chore, and nothing depressed him like a sinkful of his own dirty dishes. He'd fallen into the habit of eating out, rather than at home. He often sat at the counter instead of a booth, because the counter offered more opportunity for casual conversation. Pathetic. He hunched forward in his chair, flicked ash into the wastebasket. The chair creaked dismally. He said, "When you going to hit the place, Jack?"

"Eleven o'clock."

Bradley nodded thoughtfully. Smoke dribbled out of his nostrils.

"Who's involved?"

"Eddy Orwell. Dan Oikawa. We've got ten squad cars, fifteen uniforms, two units from the dog squad."

"That ought to do it, I guess."

"There's almost three-quarters of an acre of grounds," said Willows, a hint defensively.

The light was a little darker now, purplish in the corners of the office — turning the color of varicose veins. He was almost twice as old as Claire Parker — in three days he'd be sixty.

"Maybe I'll come along," Bradley said. "Just for the ride."

Willows gaped at him.

"You don't mind, I hope."

"Of course not," said Parker.

24

At Blanca and Chancellor Boulevard there was a loop, a turnaround for the buses that travelled up Tenth Avenue and serviced the University of British Columbia. The loop was in the shape of a half-circle, and except for the Blanca Street side, was surrounded by a windbreak of thirty-foot high cedar trees.

Ten patrol cars and an enclosed van — a paddy wagon that would be used to transport the smaller fish to the city jail at 312 Main — stood idling on the asphalt. A copse of alder and wild cherries stood at the curve of the loop that was farthest from the street, and the squad stood in darkness beneath the trees as Willows went over his plan of attack for the last time, making doubly sure everyone knew exactly what to do and when to do it.

There was nothing complex about the plan.

Gary Silk's ten-thousand square foot home had one front and one rear entrance.

A ground-level door on the east side of the house gave access to the basement.

The only way in or out of the squash courts was via the glass-enclosed walkway that connected with the house.

Willows wanted four men at the front door, three at the rear and two more at the basement entrance. Teams of two men plus a dog and handler in the front yard and behind the house, at the garden gate. Willows and Parker would take four more men into the house with them. One of the detectives, Oikawa, was armed with a riot gun.

There was another riot gun in the backyard, by the gate leading to the lane. There was tear gas if they needed it.

The last thing Willows did was run a quick equipment check,

make sure the walkie-talkies were functioning and everyone had the right frequency.

"Okay," he said at last, "let's get it over with."

The procession swung out of the bus loop. Gary Silk's multi-million-dollar oceanview home on Drummond Drive was exactly half a mile away. They'd be there in minutes.

The house was on the south side of the street, hidden behind a neatly trimmed ten-foot high boxwood hedge and an ornate, electronically controlled wrought-iron gate.

The aluminum grid of an intercom was set into one of the granite posts that flanked the gate. A fat yellow button glowed in the darkness, but there was no need to push it — the gate was wide open.

"Think they're expecting us?" said Parker.

"Let's hope not." Willows rolled down his window. The sound of crushed limestone beneath the tires seemed very loud as he drove slowly towards the house. The driveway was on the left side of the property, snaked through thin stands of deciduous trees. The trees were small and misshapen, the branches gnarled and oddly twisted, as if writhing in pain. Mushroom-shaped security lights, apparently placed at random, illuminated the trunks and lower branches, brilliant emerald patches of close-cropped lawn.

The house was about a hundred feet in from Drummond Drive. All the windows were brightly lit. The front door was wide open and a shaft of yellow light spilled across the steps and threw the risers in black shadow.

Three cars were parked in the circular driveway in front of the house — a dark green Morgan, a black Lincoln Continental and a white Cadillac. Willows pulled up behind the Caddy, turned off the Olds' engine. Car doors slammed shut behind him. A dog whined. Someone, Oikawa probably, worked the pump action of his riot gun. There were muttered voices, the soft clatter of equipment.

Willows waited by the car as the team dispersed to their positions. The men fanned across the yard, dark blue jumpsuits quickly swallowed by the darkness.

Parker had her gun in her hand. Willows started up the

sidewalk. He reached the wide front porch. There were two big clay pots full of some kind of ivy, a pair of white-painted wooden garden chairs and a matching bench that was suspended from the porch ceiling by chains and was swaying gently. A girl lay on the bench, curled up on her side, apparently asleep.

Parker went over and looked down at her. The girl's eyes were open, the pupils dilated. She was wearing an Orange Julius uniform; dark brown slacks and a matching blouse with orange trim.

"What's your name?" said Parker.

"Samantha."

"Are you all right?"

"I dunno. Ask Gary." The girl's voice was thick, slurred. Her breath smelled of gin. She rolled over on her back, closed her eyes and began to snore.

"I think I took her out once," said Oikawa. "Or maybe it was somebody just like her."

Willows pointed at one of the uniformed policemen stationed at the bottom of the steps. "Put her in a squad car and make sure somebody keeps an eye on her."

Oikawa and Parker and three uniformed cops followed Willows through the big front door, into an entrance hall as large as Parker's apartment. There were closed doors to left and right, a central hallway that led towards the rear of the house. A huge, pale green cactus stood in a ceramic pot. There was a desk with a telephone on it, and four black and white studio photographs of Gary Silk clutching a squash racket and a handful of trophies. Ahead of them, a curving stairway led to the second floor of the house. A burst of laughter floated down to them.

Willows told the three uniforms to check the ground floor of the house. He and Parker and Oikawa started up the stairs. At the landing, the spiky arms of another cactus reached out to greet them.

Gary, Frank, Pat Nash, Randall and his girlfriend Ginger were all in the den, drinking beer and smoking Kelowna Gold as they watched taped highlights of the previous year's Superbowl game on Gary's big fifty-two inch color TV. The leaded glass windows overlooking the backyard were wide open, but even so, the air was thick with the sweet, cloying scent of marijuana.

The ball was snapped.

There was a spectacular midfield collision.

"Wow," said Randall.

"It's a contact sport," said Gary. He slapped Ginger on the thigh, gave her a friendly squeeze that lasted far too long. Ginger glared at Randall, but Randall was smart enough to concentrate on the game. Frank winked at Pat Nash and Nash glanced away. The throwaway .38 Frank had given him pressed against his belly. His bladder felt as if it was about to burst. He crossed his legs, squeezed them together. He'd already left the room once, said he needed to use the toilet but had made a quick trip to Gary's bedroom.

It was Frank who finally noticed Willows and Parker standing in the doorway. He looked into the muzzle of Parker's .38 Special, then at the gold detective's shield clipped to her lapel. Willows smiled at him. He put his beer down on an inlaid rosewood coffee table, dropped the joint hissing into the glass.

"What the fuck y'do that for?" said Gary.

Frank stood up very slowly, keeping his hands away from his sides. He turned off the TV.

Gary said, "What the hell you think you're up to, Frank?"

Frank jerked his thumb at Willows and Parker. Gary's eyes widened comically. He started to get up, had second thoughts. The flight bag stuffed with five hundred thousand dollars in small bills, no consecutive serial numbers, was sitting on the sofa beside him. He put his arm around the bag. The Japanese cop pointed the riot gun at him.

Gary said, "Got a warrant?"

Parker had never met anyone before who could talk and sneer at the same time. She showed Gary the paper. Gary studied the warrant. The date and address were correct. The rest of it didn't make any sense to him at all. The lady cop took the warrant away from him. He stuffed his hands in his pockets and said, "I know my rights, and I wanna make a phone call."

There was a gas fireplace against the far wall of the room. On the mantle were several sports trophies, tiny, featureless, chrome-plated figures with rackets held high. Willows went over and took a look. The trophies were from local squash tournaments that had taken place during the past three years. Gary had three seconds and two thirds but had never taken all the marbles. At the far end of the mantle, partly hidden by an antique carriage clock, was the top half of another trophy, a player whose legs had been snapped off at the knees. Willows slipped an evidence bag out of his pocket.

"What the fuck you doing?" said Gary. He turned to Frank. "What's he doing, Frank?"

Willows dropped the trophy into the bag.

"What d'you want with that?" Gary said. He nibbled at his thumbnail. "Get me the phone, Frank."

"You can make a call when we get downtown," Willows said.

"Oh, is that right? Going downtown, are we? My lawyer's gonna like that. It's closer to his fucking office."

Willows recognized Frank from his mug shots but the guy in the tight pink leather outfit was a complete stranger to him.

"What's your name?"

"Randall."

"That's it?"

"Randall DesMoines."

"Got something with a picture on it, Randall?"

Randall had a Washington State driver's licence. He also had licences from the states of Minnesota and Iowa and Oregon, and a local licence issued to someone named Richard Clark. Randall had Clark's VISA and Mastercard as well as the licence. Credit cards were always a lot of fun, but Willows had no idea why Randall had kept the licence, since Clark was obviously white and Randall obviously wasn't. Willows turned his attention to Pat Nash.

Nash glanced at Oikawa, the riot gun. He put his hands on his head, fingers interlocked. The movement pulled his cotton windbreaker up, exposing the butt of the cheap .38. The riot gun settled on his belly. He said, "Don't shoot."

Oikawa said, "Up to you, pal."

Willows pulled the .38 from the waistband of Nash's pants. He cuffed him, hands behind his back, and then patted him down.

Nash had a .45 calibre Derringer tucked away in an ankle holster. Frank saw it and tried not to look surprised. Willows pocketed the Derringer. Nash's wallet was in his jacket pocket. He was carrying several hundred dollars in twenties and a thick sheaf of lottery tickets, but no identification.

The girl kept looking at Randall. It wasn't all that hard to figure out their relationship, but what, Willows wondered, did a hot shot like Gary want with an imported pimp and his thirty-dollar hooker?

He picked up the plastic bag full of marijuana that lay on the coffee table.

"This belong to you, Gary?"

"Fuck, no." Gary pointed at Randall DesMoines. "You better ask him about it."

"See the lady," said Randall. The hooker gave him a big smile.

Willows sensed movement behind him. Three uniformed policemen crowded into the den.

"You got 'em all," said one of the cops, a man named Keynes. "The rest of the house is empty."

"Let's take a look around," said Willows. "See what we can find." Gary Silk grinned at him.

"You remind me of somebody," said Keynes. "Cocky little bastard, a tennis player." He turned to Willows. "Can't think of the name, but you probably know who I mean, he pushes razor blades on TV."

"John McEnroe," said Willows.

"Right," said Keynes. Now he knew how you got to be a detective and wear nice clothes.

"McEnroe's a lot taller," said Frank. "And a lot nicer, too, I bet."

Gary Silk pushed off the sofa, took two quick strides across the room and dove through the open window into the backyard. Oikawa had him in his sights and then he was gone, had vanished into the darkness.

"Jesus!" said Keynes.

Parker ran to the window and looked out. She saw a blur of white scrambling across the grass towards the back fence. A police dog growled, low and guttural and very menacing.

Oikawa swept the barrel of the riot gun in a wide arc. Frank and Pat Nash and Randall and his sweetheart stood motionless as the glittering trophies arranged on the fireplace mantle.

Willows ran out of the den with Parker right behind him.

They found the dog belly up in the fishpond, blood leaking from a stab wound to the chest.

They found Gary Silk hiding in the cabbage patch, tangled up in the netting Frank had strung to keep away the birds.

"I'm Farmer McGregor," said Willows. "And you must be Peter Rabbit."

They found the .25 calibre Star that had been used to shoot Oscar Peel where Pat Nash had thought to hide it — under an oversized down pillow on Gary's custom-made kingsize water-bed. The bed had a mirrored headboard inset with a row of mother-of-pearl buttons that made it vibrate, revolve, tilt at different angles and otherwise attempt to compensate for Gary's sexual inadequacies, real and imagined.

Frank and Pat Nash and Randall DesMoines and Ginger the hooker had been herded downstairs to the living-room. Randall had the floor, was explaining how he'd salted room 318 with the hypo and the spent .22 calibre shell he'd picked up the night he'd been shot, and why he'd felt it was necessary to take Moira's body back to the Vance Hotel, instead of just rolling her up in a carpet and dumping her in an alley. When it became clear that Randall had done all this in the hope of framing whoever had shot him, Willows interrupted his monologue to show Gary Silk the murder weapon.

Gary didn't seem to take Willows seriously when he told him where the gun had been found. "Who the fuck you think you're kidding!" he yelled. Then he looked at Pat Nash, and what he saw in Nash's eyes made his face flush with blood and then turn white with rage.

"You set me up, you goddamn prick!"

"Where the hell did *that* come from?" Frank said, staring in bewilderment at the gun.

Pat Nash edged a little closer and told him how, on the night of the murder, he'd pretended to stumble and had picked up a rock and thrown it into the ocean, then stuck the Star in his back pocket. Frank grinned wryly.

Life, no matter how long you lived it, was full of surprises.

Willows was confident that the bullet retrieved from Oscar Peel's body would match the rifling on the Star. He still didn't have a motive, but he was sure he had more than he needed for a conviction. He charged Gary with second-degree murder and read him his rights, asked him if he understood what had been said.

"Fuck you," said Gary.

Willows assumed that meant yes.

There are no sidewalks on Drummond Drive, just wide, grassy, well-tended boulevards. Paterson parked his plum-colored Porsche on the grass beneath a streetlight and walked slowly down the road towards the wrought-iron gate. Limestone chips crunched beneath his feet. His heart pounded in his chest. The sky was clear and there was a cool breeze coming in from the sea, but he was sweating, short of breath, felt as if he'd run all the way across town instead of driving.

He was halfway up the driveway before he noticed the squad cars parked in front of the house. He hesitated, tripped over his own feet and at that moment a uniformed cop stepped out from behind a shrub. The cop ran his flashlight up and down the length of Paterson's body and then held the beam steady on his face.

"Is there a problem, officer?"

The officer asked him who he was and what he wanted. He reached down deep and, in a moment of inspiration, found what he was looking for.

"My name's Anthony Morgan. I'm Mr Silk's lawyer."

Paterson slipped the pigskin driving glove off his right hand, fumbled for his wallet. He handed the cop one of the business cards he'd taken from the desk in Morgan's office. The cop studied the card for a long moment and then spoke into his walkie-talkie. There was a lengthy pause, a burst of static.

"You can't go into the house. You want to see him, you're gonna have to wait until after he's booked."

Paterson nodded. He cleared his throat. "Hey," he said, "do I look as if I'm in a hurry?"

He held out his hand. The cop returned the card. He turned and walked stiff-legged down the driveway, past the big iron gates. He reached the road, took a few more steps, and let go of the briefcase.

Eighty million dollars' worth of heroin and the .22 calibre Ruger that had fired the spent shell found by Jack Willows at the death scene at the Vance Hotel hit the asphalt with a dull thud.

Paterson climbed into the Porsche and started the engine. It was time to take the long ride home.

A quarter of an hour later, Willows and Parker and a dozen uniformed policemen led Gary Silk and his entourage down the steps of the house on Drummond Drive towards the cluster of waiting squad cars.

They were halfway down the steps when Willows saw Tracy Peel walking across the lawn towards them. In the darkness, he thought at first that she was the girl in the Orange Julius uniform they'd found sleeping on the front porch.

Pat Nash saw his cousin and was stunned. He stopped dead in his tracks. Tracy'd asked him where he was going that night. Fool that he was, he'd told her. The cop behind him stumbled and cursed, grabbed him by the arm and pulled hard, dragged him down the steps.

Tracy strolled across the driveway, past the squad cars and Gary's Cadillac. She reached into her purse.

Willows saw the gun come up. He yelled a warning, snatched at his revolver. A button tore loose from his jacket and rolled slowly down the stairs.

Tracy was very close now, no more than a dozen steps away. Pat Nash kneed Gary in the stomach and then head-butted him head over heels down the steps. Tracy Peel got off her first shot. Dirty orange flame spouted from the muzzle of her dead husband's .45. The recoil almost made her drop the weapon.

Frank grunted, clutched his stomach and dropped to one knee.

"Not him!" yelled Nash. His hands were cuffed behind his back. He jerked his chin towards Gary, not realizing that's who she'd been shooting at in the first place.

A cop ran down the steps directly at Tracy, into her line of fire. He was yelling at her but all she could hear was the heavy boom of the gun, the pounding of her heart. The .45 lurched in her hand. A bullet smacked into the stone wall of the house.

Willows had her in his sights. He'd never shot a woman before. She was maybe ten feet away. Time slowed right down to a crawl. He thought about the way she'd looked on the chesterfield in the basement suite on Brock Street, her baby cradled in her arms as it suckled at her breast. Both of them expressionless, watching him. The barrel of the .45 swung towards him. She wasn't looking at him, probably didn't even see him. A part of his mind registered that all she wanted was Gary, she probably didn't even see him, was going to shoot right through him. Time sped up.

Willows cried out.

The .45 exploded in his face.

Willows shot Tracy Peel in the chest.

Parker, standing so close to Willows that they were touching, fired twice. Tracy Peel staggered sideways. Willows kept seeing the baby, couldn't bring himself to shoot again. Oikawa stepped in front of him. Parker fired a third round. Tracy Peel, hit four times, fell to her knees. As she was falling, she yanked the trigger one last time.

Gary Silk regained his feet. He watched, fascinated, as the cops pumped round after round into the woman who was trying to kill him.

He saw everything but her last shot, the one that hit him.

Blood sprayed from his ears and nostrils and mouth, the back of his head. He thrust his right arm straight out in front of him and then toppled over and all five foot six inches of him hit the granite steps and lay still.

In a way, Gary's theory of gunshot wounds had proved correct. Under certain circumstances, catching a bullet didn't hurt at all.

Oikawa got to Tracy Peel first. He pried the .45 out of her hand.

Frank sat cross-legged on the stairs, clutching his belly, blood leaking from between splayed fingers. A Siamese cat was licking his face. Frank looked as if he wanted to burst into tears.

Pat Nash stared into the void. He was thinking about the way Gary Silk had taken the head shot and then, dead on his feet, thrust out his arm as if wanting to shake hands. If Gary'd gone straight to hell, had he made it home before his body'd hit the steps? Had that hand reached out to press the flesh with Oscar Peel? Nash watched Willows apply mouth-to-mouth to Tracy Peel. Gary Silk lay on his side. The bullet had hit him just above the right eye. Little waterfalls of blood ran down the steps. Nash dipped his shoe and smeared blood across Gary's nice white pants. It wasn't enough. It wasn't nearly enough. He kicked Gary in the ribs, sent him tumbling off the steps and into an azalea bush. Branches snapped. A burst of shiny red petals fluttered lightly to the ground. A bald guy taking pictures yelled something at Nash. The cat ministering to Frank lifted its head and skittered up the steps and disappeared into the house. The night air shuddered with the thin screech of sirens. Somebody shoved Nash in the small of the back and he stumbled and then regained his balance and started down the steps.

Tracy was staring up at the big black bowl of the sky, her face, what he could see of it, pale and empty. Nash yelled at her to hold on. The cop who had him in an armlock said, "Shut the fuck up, you'll wake the goddamn neighbors." Nash grinned at him. Tracy was a tough cookie — he was sure she'd pull through okay. Frank had killed her husband and Gary had ordered it done. She got herself a hot shot lawyer and an all-male jury, she'd be out in eighteen months, two years max.

The cop gave him a boost up into the paddy wagon. He sat down on a metal bench. The door slammed shut, steel on steel, plunging him into darkness.

A squad car tore chunks out of the lawn as it backed out of the driveway, making room for the ambulance.

Parker pulled Willows away from Tracy Peel. One of the ambulance attendants slapped an oxygen mask across her face. He ripped her blouse open. She'd taken four hits, all of them potentially lethal. He checked her pulse. Another night without a miracle.

And in the spacious back seat of Willows' gleaming black 1943 Oldsmobile, Inspector Homer Bradley, revolver cradled uselessly in his lap, shut his weary eyes and dreamed of brighter and much greener days.

25

Tuesday night, the sixth of September.

Jack Willows sat cross-legged on his living-room floor, a dismantled graphite Maryat fly reel laid out in front of him on a sheet of yesterday's paper. He'd stripped the line from the reel, and it lay in loose coils upon the carpet.

Izaak Walton had used a fly line made of twisted strands of horsehair — preferably from the tail of a stallion. Towards the end of the eighteenth century, lines were made of silk saturated in oil in a small vacuum and then, to achieve a harder, more impervious surface, baked in an oven for ten hours at one hundred and fifty degrees Fahrenheit.

Modern lines are made of synthetic fibres with a plastic coating. The line on the carpet was a single taper floater with a sixty-foot head and braided nylon core. It had been designed for salt-water use. Willows planned to spend the next couple of days in his waders, fishing the coastal estuaries for sea-run cutthroat trout.

The buzzer rang. He drank some Cutty, continued to clean and grease the reel. The buzzer sounded again. He unfolded his legs and stood up and went over to the intercom.

Parker.

He buzzed her in and went over and opened the door, returned to his reel and his drink. A few moments later he heard the elevator's rising drone and then the hushed murmur of the elevator doors sliding open and Parker's footsteps in the hall.

She was wearing black cords, a white blouse beneath a sleeveless black cashmere sweater. She turned slowly around, a pirouette, and said, "Nice outfit?"

"Terrific."

"You don't think the pants are too tight?"

"Maybe just a little."

"Thanks a lot."

He began to reassemble the reel. Parker crouched down beside him. He caught the fragrant, earthy scent of her perfume. She smelled the whisky. He fitted the two halves of the reel together and spun the handle. The ratchet clicked smoothly.

Parker sat down beside him on the carpet. Their knees touched and she moved slightly away, so there was a gap between them of perhaps a quarter of an inch.

"Know what I think?"

"Almost never," said Willows.

"I believe that deep down inside, there's a part of us that no one else can ever touch. And that when it comes right down to it, we're all alone, each and every one of us. There are times when I think about that and have a very hard time dealing with it. Do you have any idea what I'm talking about, Jack?"

Willows didn't look up, wouldn't meet her eye.

"I called you all weekend long," said Parker. "I left a dozen messages. Monday morning, you weren't at your desk. Bradley told me you'd phoned in sick."

She paused for a moment, decided to take the plunge.

"She call you?"

"Who?"

"Sheila," said Parker. "Your goddamn wife, who the hell do you think I'm talking about?"

"No, not yet."

"It's September the sixth, Jack. The first day of school and your kids are still in Toronto. You'd think if she was going to call, she'd have done it by now."

Willows started winding the fly line back on to the reel. He went slowly so the loose coils wouldn't tangle. The ratchet clicked off the seconds.

"Doing anything this evening?"

"Not really."

Parker stood up, walked into the bathroom. She left the door open. The shower thundered. A few minutes later Willows heard the soft pad of her bare feet on the carpet as she went into the bedroom. He put the reel away in its soft leather case. The bedsprings creaked.

In the kitchenette, the refrigerator throbbed and hummed and then the cycle ended and the apartment was impossibly quiet, impossibly still.

She had been lying on her belly, but when Willows entered the room she turned on her side, facing him. He knelt on the floor beside the bed. She reached out to him, put her arms around his neck and drew him close. His fingers traced a constellation of tiny beauty marks on the perfect curve of her hip. Her skin was smooth and firm, cool to the touch. He travelled down the length of her, a long and languorous journey.

He kissed her eyebrows, the bridge of her nose, her ears, her cheeks, her neck. He felt the hurried thump of her pulse beneath his lips.

A jumbled collage of his children playing and working and laughing and crying swept across his vision, and was swept away.

Parker's eyes were dark, liquid. He kissed her lightly on the mouth and for the first time in a very long time, slipped outside of himself and was lost.

In the soft pink light of dawn, Parker gave Willows a present, a small box wrapped in gold paper and garnished with a bow.

"What's this?"

"Open it."

Willows fumbled with the ribbon, lost patience and snapped it with his fingers.

She'd given him a Richard Wheatley dry fly box made of brushed aluminum. He opened the lid. Inside were six small compartments, each about an inch square, with a hinged lid of clear plastic and a spring that made the lid pop open when a tiny lever was pressed. The box held about two dozen flies and it was full.

"Very romantic."

"Well, you're a pretty romantic guy."

"Who chose the patterns?"

"The clerk helped."

Willows snapped the box shut. "Thank you, Claire."

Parker smiled. Rainbow in a snowstorm. His heart leapt.